I0566594

Hysteria 6

Winning short stories, flash fiction and poems from the
Hysteria 2017 Writing Competition

The Hysterectomy Association.

Edited by Linda Parkinson-Hardman

Hysteria 6

Published by: The Hysterectomy Association

ISBN: 978-0-9956957-9-5

A catalogue record for this book is available from The British Library.

Telephone: 0843 289 2142

Website: www.hysteriauk.co.uk

ABOUT THE HYSTERIA WRITING COMPETITION

Hysteria is an annual writing competition for women only; it opens on the 1st April each year and closes at midnight on the 31st August. You can find out more about the competition, including rules and guidelines for entries on the Hysterectomy Association website about the next competition at: *www.hysteriauk.co.uk*.

Acknowledgements

The competition and this anthology wouldn't have been possible without the support and help of all the following people.

This book is dedicated to them and to the users of the Hysterectomy Association.

Thank you. Linda Parkinson-Hardman (editor).

Judges

Short Stories:	Flash Fiction:	Poetry:
• Celine Domenech	• Damhnait Monaghan	• Josianne Barrette
• Jenny Roman	• Ingrid Jendrzejewski	• Shaheen Hussain
• Natasha Bland	• Marie Gethins	• Maya Pieris
• Liz Berg	• Becky Danks	• Susan Borgersen
	• Ann Abineri	• Janet Lees

FOREWORD

I love words. I love the way they invoke an emotion or an image in my head. And, when they are combined in a masterpiece of prose or poetry, can literally make my heart sing.

We should never underestimate the ability of the words we use, the stories we write and the poems we share to change our perspective and, even in some amazing instances, our world.

I'm always awed by the capacity our Hysteria writing competition entrants have to use language in a way that creates so much meaning. And I am humbled, knowing it's unlikely I'll ever be able to create such evocative cadence, rhythm and insight myself.

My congratulations go to everyone who appears in the anthology, you are the best of an excellent bunch.

Linda

Contents

FLASH FICTION

The Flash Fiction category is open to entries with a maximum word count of 250 words. These ultra-short stories needed to be complete and give the reader the satisfaction of not being left hanging.

Flash fiction is fictional work of extreme brevity, that still offers the author and reader the benefit of character and plot development.

ADVICE FROM OUR FLASH FICTION JUDGES

Damhnait Monaghan

@Downith

Thank you to Linda for giving me the opportunity to act as a flash judge in this year's Hysteria Competition and well done to all of you who entered this year. You can't win it, if you're not in it, right?

Here are my three top tips for the next competition you enter. Let's call them the three R's.

RULES - Familiarise yourself with the rules and guidelines and make sure you comply with them. Word count, theme, font: give the organisers what they want.

READ – Read, read, read. It sounds trite, but you learn so much about writing through reading. Read for enjoyment, but also to see what works. What made this story excellent? Why didn't you like that one? You can also learn about formatting, which leads me to one of my punctuation bugbears: these days it's one space at the end of a sentence, not two.

REVISE – Some of the flash fiction entries I read gave the impression they were dashed off and sent in without so much as a second glance. Punctuation errors, sloppy writing and lack of flow were obvious in some of the entries. When you have a draft you're happy with, put it aside for a few days. When you go back to it, read it out loud. If a sentence sounds awkward when read aloud, it will be awkward when read. In flash fiction every word counts, so choose the best possible ones. Edit and polish and edit again. Only then should you send it in.

Becky Danks

www.beckydanks.com

For me, a good piece of flash fiction is all about the detail. Every word counts. The best flash fiction is like a work of art. When asked how he created his masterpieces, Michelangelo said: 'I saw the angel in the marble and carved until I set him free.' This is what flash fiction writers need to do with words. They carve up sentences to reveal the exquisite detail within.

I particularly enjoy reading character-focused pieces exploring emotional experiences and making observations the reader can relate to. The story should feel natural and not forced. A sudden twist at the end isn't necessary, I like the drama to build slowly throughout the piece.

Careful editing is essential. It's a good idea to write the story, edit it and then, if you have time, leave it in a drawer for a couple of weeks. When you go back to it, edit it again. The time away helps to see the work with a fresh pair of eyes and makes the editing process a little easier.

Marie Gethins

@MarieGethins

I thoroughly enjoyed reading the variety of subjects and styles in this collection of submissions. Unfortunately, a large number did not have the elements I look for in a strong flash, but fell into what I would term 'vignettes'. They detailed an episode and were one-note in content. While flash encompasses a great variety of approaches, I think it's strength is that much of it is off the page. Subtext that resonates long after reading, as well as subtle meanings that require puzzling out are elements I look for in an ideal flash. While a scene may be interesting, it needs a deeper thread to make it a flash. Your title can be a key ingredient in adding information, honing language to fundamentals, and skilled use of metaphors are all ways to add that extra layer. Flash lends itself to the twist ending, but you really have to earn it.

Ingrid Jendrzejewski

@LunchOnTuesday

It was an honour and a privilege to read each and every flash submitted to this year's competition – every single one had something to admire.

The ones that have stayed with me longest – the ones I keep coming back to even now – are the ones that accomplish that holy grail of storytelling: the surprising yet inevitable ending.

It's difficult enough to craft an effective twist or punchline, and I admire writers who can do so. However, I more than anything, I love the pieces that stand up to reading after reading, even after I know the ending. These are the pieces that give me something unexpected – be it plot points, language, or imagery – but that earn their twist; every subsequent reading has something new and rich to offer, yet I can't imagine the story ending any other way.

My congratulations go to all the brilliant writers included in this anthology.

YOU DON'T HAVE TO TALK ABOUT YOUR DADDY IN COUNSELLING IF YOU DON'T WANT TO

Stephanie Hutton

@tiredpsych

Jupiter is the stormiest planet. It has weather patterns that change quickly, so you never know what swirly clouds might hide.

It is separated from Earth by the asteroid belt - hard and dangerous to reach.

Jupiter spins fast on its axis, so each day is short. There wouldn't be much time to spend there on a daytrip. But if it raged, at least you could start the next day again quickly, forget it had happened at all.

Funny thing is, its year is longer than Earth's. Jupiter takes ages to come back where it started. It's probably not worth waiting around for.

Jupiter has four major moons. But actually, it has so many other moons all over the place that the major moons aren't special.

Three Earths can fit inside Jupiter's great red spot. So even if Earth got hot and fiery like it might explode, it would disappear into that red hole and you wouldn't be able to see it at all.

Astronomers call Jupiter a failed star. Maybe that's why it's so angry and stormy. It could never become as beautiful as the sun.

You might think you don't like the sound of this planet; it's too fierce, too far. Trouble is, it has a powerful gravitational force that objects just get drawn to. Then they circle around and around Jupiter forever, never getting any closer, forgetting where they'd wanted to go.

Rachel Hughes

@RachelAudreyH

In the weeks we planned her bedroom, all we did was discuss colours. Pink – but then were we really those parents who subscribe to stereotypical gender specific colours? Blue – but then were we really those annoying statement parents? Green – but neither of us even like that colour. We still hadn't even decided on a name when the cramps started. We were at B&Q buying white paint. I was supposed to have six weeks to finish decorating. She was born yellow. They taped dark glasses to her face. They knitted tiny white tubes around her body. For the first twenty-four hours of her life she was indigo under UV rays. She twisted and wriggled in the light like she was kicking water out of a bath. We called her Plum.

THE TRUTH BEHIND THE LABELS

Gaynor Kate Jones

@jonzeywriter

On Thursdays, we're made to wear labels with our name and favourite hobby on. It seems we can't be trusted to just socialise normally like functioning adults. Mine currently says 'needle felting' because I'm not sure the luncheon club is quite the place to reveal my penchant for a bit of mild S and M, what with all the weak hearts and high blood pressure.

I dutifully mingle, scanning the other labels on display while imagining the truth behind each one.

David, 'amateur dramatics'. He cosplays at the weekend. His lycra Spider-Man suit has seen a lot of wear, but the ladies still seem to like it.

Margaret, 'baking'. She batch cooks huge mounds of marijuana-laced brownies to sell outside the student union. Tops up the pension, after all.

Edmund, 'keeping fit'. Every Friday, he dons a rubber mask and the most miniscule shorts you've ever seen to battle it out in an oily wrestling ring.

Rose, 'romance novels'. She writes pornographic Gardener's World fan fiction on a secret online forum. Her pen name is Thorny Bush.

I'm so engaged in my daydreams, I barely notice the woman smiling in front of me.

Underneath 'Lesley' she's written 'sky diving'.

'Crikey, Lesley, how do they fit the Zimmer in the plane?'

She chuckles.

'I hate being put on the spot. And it sounds more exciting than shopping.'

I picture the latex-riddled catalogue hidden in my nightstand.

'Well, Lesley, I guess that depends on what you're buying!'

THE BEACH

Amanda Speed

Her eyes follow the shimmering sweep of the land curve. She licks her lips. Her eyes are dry, a mermaid who cannot cry. Beached. Pine trees, wispy dancers between sand and cliff, give out a scent mixing with whiffs of sea.

Yes, yes, she says, as she places her toes into the edge of the ocean. Water shimmers with thousands of slivers of sunlight. Foam thoughts bubble up from underneath, still wet. She leaves her footprints across the empty sand.

She just wants to lay her head on the shoulder of the sea. To be taken into the arms of the world. But, no, another thought bubbles up. Her children, smaller, running laughing and screaming into the cold waves and then laughing out again, innocence and joy.

She is wet to the knees. Shivers climb up. It caresses her skin, this admirer, this velvet water. A salt water caress, Japanese green. Her body begins to sing. What is it to be a woman? It is to sing at the touch of the sea.

She takes her back for a boat. Her ears fill with water lapping and pulling at pebbles in the unrolling waves. She lets herself slide. She is carried on this infinitely fine skin that contains the force of the sea. Moonish, like the planet which reflects the rhythms of her body and inflames her infinite nights. Woman.

She feels, floating there languorously, that she is totally empty, weightless, no longer there.

SURVIVAL TACTICS

Frances Gapper

www.francesgapper.co.uk

They've got a name for me and I know what it is. In my last office, where most of us took unusual forms, colleagues affectionately dubbed me Octo. But here no love, here no rescuing tide. I'm beach-stranded, poked at by cruel kids.

The boss asked us to brainstorm, what single thing are we not doing that we could or should do? Let's go round the table. People suggested updating our spreadsheets; online surveys to gauge customer opinion; away days for staff training. Answers pathetic in their timidity and caution. Marina? He blinked at me. I think, I said, we don't touch each other enough. Not a squeak in response to this expression of my heartfelt belief. We should tidy our desks said the next person and they all clapped. Excellent!

I long for intimate contact. Often I reach over a partition, or under a desk where computer wires make nobbles in the grimy carpet, to tickle the back of someone's neck, explore the whorls of their ear or caress the crease of a bare knee. My friendly fondlings are slapped at like mosquitoes. My tentacles gesture in the dry air.

Why are you here, a young male colleague interrupted me while I was training him in Illustrator. Well, the oceans are polluted and clogged with bits of plastic. And though my official retirement age is horizon-drawn as a Kent coast ebbtide, I'm conscious of the need to provide for when I'm ancient and stink of fish.

Heads Off

Sally Page

@SalnPage

'Get the biggest you can. Heads off.'

John has got his assignment. It's for local news and is about the Obesity Crisis. Boring. And a bit embarrassing. But work is work. He heads off to town with his camera.

Josie is out for the first time in years. Shopping with her sister. She's lost five stone now but still has seven to go. She buys a top that fits, a lipstick and a big pineapple. They stop for lunch at the wholefood café and walk a long way before Josie says goodbye to her sister and heads off home, feeling great.

John's finished. He's in the pub. Three pints and some chips.

Josie's having a jacket potato and beans. She's planning a walk tomorrow. Wondering about the weather, she switches on the local news.

4Ever

Jayne Martin

Those of us left who still bore memories gathered in the parking lot and sang the school anthem as the wrecking ball closed in on the old stone structure. Few of us could argue that it was time. Transients and bored teens had been breaking into the place for years.

Somewhere in the pile of discarded desks was one with "JM + GR 4ever" carved on its blond wood face. I'd used the pointed end of the heart-shaped pendant you'd given me for my 16th birthday. Two years later, I'd enter Ball State and you'd ship off to someplace called Vietnam that none of us had ever heard of. The boy who returned was as hollowed out as these ancient hallways. Still, it's good to see you here today.

My husband's arm slips around my waist. I lean into his side, grateful for the good life we've been given, while my hand finds its way to the delicate gold chain encircling my neck even now. I wonder if you ever think of me.

TRAIN RIDE

Kay Rae Chomic

www.kayraechomic.com

Rayleen rode the train west to Chicago sitting in a red-cushioned booth surrounded by cherry wood paneling. Hours shy of her 21st birthday, she launched her dream plan—to rent an apartment from Aunt Francine in Chicago, tend bar at Uncle Frank's pub, walk on the Lakefront Trail in the hair-whipping, lip-chapping, word-swallowing wind that Lake Michigan spawned. Her stomach fluttered. Rayleen searched for the Red Vines in her over-stuffed backpack.

While sucking on cherry sweetness, Rayleen looked out the window into backyards of clapboard houses. She saw stray dogs, men throwing horseshoes, kids on swings, skateboarders on quarter pipe ramps, lovers in hammocks. The train's whistle blew into and out of every small town on the way.

A red smudge of a barn caught her attention. She twisted in her seat to glimpse more of it. Red barns always made her smile. Rayleen's mouth opened slightly as if to say something, or as if to take in a tongue with a kiss. Her first kiss—in a red barn, with a girl. With a girl lying In a loft of fresh hay. With a girl who had worn ersatz pearls and cowgirl boots and a Wrangler skirt. She had reduced Rayleen's fear to a size she could swallow. That girl, Celia, did for her what no boy had done since.

Rayleen hoped to meet other girls like Celia in the big city.

A STILL, SMALL POINT OF REFERENCE

Fiona J. Mackintosh

@fionajanemack

Each morning as the egg-yolk sun rises down the beach, I see you start your vigil, coffee cup in hand, staring out to where the sea's a silver dazzle, where every whitecap, every diving bird deceives the eye.

As the days stretch their arc across the water, I watch you watching the horizon, your feet up on the railing, binoculars around your neck. Since I first kissed you long ago in freshman year, I've learned to love your doggedness, the torque of it, the thing that drives you on when other people fall away.

But I see how much you miss in all that striving. Ebbing waves laced with tiny bubbles, the jerky strut of sandpipers across the tight wet sand that's flecked with foam. Humming insects in the dune grass, the dart of lizards on sun-warmed wood. The taste of salt against your mouth, and the sweet drag of fingertips on peeling summer skin.

Even on the epic day they crested near the shore, even as you ran along the beach beside them, when you felt a sonic pulse of kinship pass from them to you and back again, it was over in a few short minutes as the pod outpaced your human stride, the black fins dwindling down the shore and out of sight. And you were left with nothing but the surf booming in and hissing out, the long waves frilling round your ankles, already wanting more.

MATCHMAKER

Louise Mangos

@LouiseMangos

A shift of the eyes. A flutter of lashes. A beat of the heart. A split second. That's all it takes.

The buzzard flies off a fence post, its pale brown body ghosting on the mist. Mottled wings dip towards a mash of flattened carrion glued to the road. Temptation eclipses a careful perception, and it alights with tail feathers fanned in excited anticipation.

Sarah, calculating how long the sirloin will take to roast in the oven for her husband and the kids when she arrives home, swerves to avoid the bird.

Increasing velocity and engine vibration relents the oncoming driver's wallet from his dashboard. It bounces off the central console, and slips to the floor. Peter searches at his feet near the pedals, fingers patting dried mud, pieces of grit and stale crisp crumbs. As he reaches further forward under the column, his movement hauls the steering wheel imperceptibly sideways.

There is opportunity for a good match. Sarah's household stress with her fractious children, and her husband's numerous business trips. Peter's handsome looks, carefree attitude, and his desire for no strings attached.

The head-on encounter is perfectly synchronised.

They will not meet again.

POETRY

The poetry category sought entries which have a maximum of 20 lines, not including spaces. Many of our entries followed a strict rule of either four or five line stanzas, but a few challenged this convention.

Poetry is a piece of writing in which the expression of feelings and ideas is given intensity by particular attention to diction (sometimes involving rhyme), rhythm, and imagery.

Janet Lees

janetlees.weebly.com

Because they give you a deadline to focus on, competitions are one way of fine-tuning poems that need fine-tuning. Some people groan at the word 'editing', but this can be one of the most rewarding parts of the creative process. There's a stubbornly enduring perception out there that a poem is something you rattle off in moments, a 'Ta-da!' kind of thing. Not in my experience. One of my poems went through more than 35 drafts before I was happy with it (this is an extreme case, but I'd typically go through at least five).

Suddenly getting a breakthrough on a line your gut tells you just isn't right, or finding the exact word you didn't even know you were looking for, is a joyous experience. Poetry is a distillation of our thought, feeling and experience; every single element of a poem has to work for its living. When it comes to competitions, your title and first line in particular need to work as hard as they can. There are lots of great tips out there – google poets you admire for their advice on writing for competitions – but above all, submit your best poems; the ones you have crafted and grafted over, the ones that have lived in your heart for a while.

Maya Pieris

Writing is such a personal and private affair with a public face attached and it takes courage with a touch of self-awareness to take the private world into the public one. When asked "who do you write for" my answer is always "myself" and if others enjoy then well and good. And I often think "never again" and then worms of words work themselves into the head and the process starts again. Invariably I plunder myself and my experiences and feelings but it is important to be aware of the unseen, unknown audience even if, like me, you do write primarily for yourself- the experience has to have a wider perspective to link into the lives and thoughts of others. I would, however, like to applaud all the entrants and also the other judges-it was a first for me and a lot harder than I had imagined it would be. The entrants have done us proud and I hope we judges have done so for you.

Being critical and critiquing are very different beasts and I suspect most of us are more practised at the former! There were some poems that stood out as really good and some howlers which showed up the importance of being read and critiqued before sending but not everyone wants this "slash and burn" done to their work. But being creative does take hard work though people think it mysteriously "happens" and taking on board opinions is hard. And in the end it's the writer's decision!

Josianne Barrett

@JosiannBarrett

To me, theme is key. The judges see the same themes repeatedly and will strongly respond to originality. If you are more at ease writing about what you know - and that's okay - then you will have to showcase the uniqueness of your voice to make your poem about a common experience stand out and reach readers in new ways.

Shaheen Hussain

www.poetrybysheenapoetrybyname.com

Being new to judging Hysteria competition gave me a real insight into the world of judging poetry. There was a real eclectic mix of beautiful poetry, full of descriptive language which gave me something to really get stuck into. However, at times, I felt I had to be quite ruthless

24

because at the end of the day this was a competition. The standard was high but a few really stood out to for me—may the deserving one win!

Jane Doe #503

Laura Potts

@thelauratheory_

Yes. Back then, I was child of a garden and pavement
end. When homestead old was forest and fire, and high
were the gold robes of fields which rose to my run, some
say I tore up the moors. On that cold morning and grey,

before day burst down a valley now lost (I cross
myself and pray), I lay in the grass like a child of light.
The stars said yesterday's night lived on, but gone
were the fawns which shaped the hill. Out and away,

still, I remember the scrap of a scream on the wind.
After that? Nil. But spilt down the river my girlhood blood
when he came with his bird-wet skin, portraits of women
gone thin in his eyes. My cries are yesterday's

echo. No. To red-slit fig he pressed his teeth, gum
to a garden in infancy green and only the hills to hear.
Wind-sneer spat at the curl of my ear on that black-flat
ground, when pale were the globes of clay

in my eyes. He rolled them skullwards once, twice. Some
nights, the shy face of moon makes a bruise in the sky
high-hung in a field where no wildfowl graze, cries for
my last-gasp fire of youth. Yes. I have seen better days.

FRUIT SALAD

Gwen Sayors

www.gwensayers.com

After Edvard Munch

A loquat's bruised flesh
holds two stones. Bananas
yield as she peels. Her knife
slips when she splits
an apple. Fruit escapes
her crimson grip and rolls.
She reaches, knocks the bowl.
Glass splinters on cold tiles.

She swirls blood and peach pulp
on the countertop, sculpts
a pear-shaped face from mashed
banana. Loquat stones gaze, dazed.
Her wedding ring open-mouths
a scream. She signs in lime.

THE TWO FRIDAS

Zara Bosman

Instagram: zarajbosman

I wear a white dress
Lace punctured with a hole by my rib-cage
From which my heart drinks from a vein
Connected to the heart of my split self
dressed in black, funeral shroud
An umbilical connection between me and me
I forget which is which
Or who is who

The one 'I' holds a pair of scissors dipped in red
Which drip drip drips onto the lace
A sinister star where the vein has been snipped
The other 'I' fingers a photo of you
Locket of my love
Into which the vein feeds

I wear my heart like a lead medallion
Heavy and pulsating on my chest for all to see
Veins that twist blue like electrical cords
A raw socket

Put your finger in it
I dare you

My Mother's Spoon

Nadia Arbach

@NadiaArbach

is engraved with admonitions
shape up, control yourself
do you really think you should?
its cold handle's edged with pearls
each one an eye

my mother's spoon
is a blind automaton
slipping velvet mouthfuls in
until it scrapes the bottom
of the bowl

my mother's spoon
is a funhouse mirror
its concave shape reverses and distorts
tarnishing her reflection
with uncertainty

my mother has forged me a spoon
she has polished it, hallmarked it
inscribed it with *be good*
I have brought it to my mouth
many times

A WOMAN OF THE ROAD

Robyn Curtis

robyncurtispoet.wordpress.com

I carry my home in carrier bags
because walls don't bend
tend to be solid; nights are cold,
and wet is worse, but lonely? No,
the hordes keep me company.

I take a line for a walk
each day; night's even better,
I thread a silver trail in the dark
criss-cross other snail wanderers.

Once I went in the museum of Unnatural History;
the winged things they'd pinned
through the heart, sliced
into thin drawers.

Once they put me in a flat
on the nineteenth floor
slid me in a layer of concrete
shelving; I flew out first night,
wings intact.

Everyone wonders what's in the bags.
Wouldn't you like to know?

CAUGHT

Victoria Richards

www.victoriarichards.co.uk

I see you in Instagram squares, hair long, lank
against your collar, pinned with fine gold intent.
Your careful stubble, eyes burning
with filtered nonchalance,
thin, gawky frame hidden in denim –
trying to hide in denim. On your shoulder
a tattoo of a fox, or bear, or a fox
pretending to be a bear.
I never cared enough to commit
your face to memory,
never thought about your lips. I saw
your self-indulgent poetry as self-indulgent poetry.
But I remember the way your hands felt, slippery
as scales across my belly, my back, as I
pretended to drink, fresh life spawning secret inside me.
I ducked and dived like trout to get away
from your fish hook smile, those
shark teeth, nibbling
at my skin, but I
couldn't swim fast enough.

SON

Moira Garland

@moiragauthor

Another year, now
he's more than my size, measures
up, way beyond me in Maths.

This afternoon I listen:
he reckons there's a great white egret
stretched as if to leave.
He calculates the antlers of the deer
that turns, runs
into the green wood
looking for another year, and another.

Marie Chambers

www.mariechambers.net

Wild Bill died in a car crash
on old Ingram Road near Crider's
where he used to dance a wicked two step
with Amelia Rodriquez and her Rolls Royce hips.

"May the lord be with thee and me in our absence"
prays the headstone his mother bought.

Birds of porcelain
A Rottweiler figurine
An old toy truck rusting in place
Christmas poinsettias bleached pink as Valentines
She steps past seasons of plastic flora
over the graves of infants and hipsters to bring him coffee.

Identical brown cups with white rims
sit caddy cornered near the B in Wild Bill
on a cement slab no bigger than a small closet
where she convenes with what's left of him to talk.

"Do you want a little cross? Or a Jesus?" she repeats
towards the shadow of an elm tree decked with wind chimes.

Without a hint of wind the chimes begin to sing.

Tape Measure

Christine Griffin

Today I found it coiled beneath a bush,
clotted with leaves and soil
next to his tiny glove.

Months it's been there.
I've had no need of it in my inching progress
from that day to this.

That gentle autumn day smelling of mist and leaves,
he brought his plastic tools
to fix my sagging gate.

As he played, we chatted
you and I, contemplating the new life within you
waiting for the spring.

Silence drew us out.
A trail of tools pulled us forward.
A screwdriver by the rose bush
led to a wrench on the rockery

and a hammer
and his hat
floating on the pond.

While I Sleep

Marie Dolores

www.mariedolores.com

They steal things.
Strand by strand the colour from my hair.
Those that resist are plucked whole.
Some retreat, only to reappear on my chin.

They try to steal my skin.
That battle I win,
but the tug-of-war leaves jowls,
turkey wattle, and underarm sag.

Gone are bits of meniscus from knees,
cartilage from hips
leaving bone to grate on bone.

Sometimes they leave things.
Nothing I want.
Extra pudding on each thigh,
quilt batting around my middle,
fluid injections for aches to greet me when I wake.

Avoiding sleep doesn't help.
A simple blink is enough
to sketch ocular roadmaps,
shade dark circles.

SHORT STORIES

The short story category is for entries of up to 2,000 words, not including the title. The short story genre is a staple of writing competitions the world over and many writers will hone their skills in this medium before venturing into the world of longer fiction.

A short story is something that can be read in a single sitting. According to Wikipedia, the written short story emerged from the tradition of oral storytelling in the 17th century.

ADVICE FROM OUR SHORT STORY JUDGES

Celine Domenech

http://fluffandpoops.com

I have three tips to help you write great stories people will enjoy reading.

Take the readers on a journey. From an imaginative plot to a cunning twist at the end, there are many ways to transform what would be a cliché into an exciting journey. First ideas are often a déjà vu: refine them to create an engaging story.

Read your story aloud before you submit. You want a natural flow. Long words might sound literary but they interrupt the story if inserted awkwardly. The same argument is valid for complex sentences, especially if you don't use enough punctuation.

Use relatable feelings. Characters are emotions' catalysts. But if they don't inspire the right emotion to your readers (such as annoyance instead of empathy), your story falls flat. It's a difficult exercise for short texts so you want to gather feedback from trusted friends before your submit.

Jenny Roman

jennyroman.wordpress.com

Judging the short story category this year was a humbling experience - there are so many good writers out there! Having said that, in order to make it to the short list, your story has to be more than good. The stories that jumped out were those where the writing was assured but not pretentious, where the characters did not feel like characters at all, but fascinating people with their own motivations and frustrations.

They were neither too obvious, nor so opaque as to leave the reader wondering what was going on. Above all, they were proper stories, written about something meaningful, with a beginning, a middle and a satisfying (and sometime surprising) end.

There are several that will stick in my mind for a long time to come - not all of which made the final short list - so thank you for the opportunity to read your work; it was a real pleasure.

STILL LIFE

Lindsay Bamfield

lindsaybamfield.blogspot.co.uk

'Are you familiar with her work?' asks someone standing near me. I turn from studying the painting, but he's already moved on, pausing for an obligatory few seconds in front of each exhibit.

The gallery is small, minimalist, light with off-white walls and pale wood flooring. Not the sort of place I associate with Reda. In spite of what my father predicted, she has amounted to something after all: the Reda Martin Retrospective. I glance at the glossy brochure in my hand with a picture of her taken, I guess, around the time I visited her.

I was nine when I met my Aunt Reda. I knew about her only because the family album displayed grainy black and white photographs of her with my father when they were children. She was absent from the photos of my parents' wedding and my christening. My parents rarely spoke of her; there was always disapproval in the set of their mouths and I learned not to ask for fear of being reprimanded for prying. Adults had private matters, my mother often said, that were not children's business.

'Let Reda see the child,' I once heard Granny plead but my parents were adamant in their refusal. When I next stayed with Granny alone, I asked about Reda but was told little more than Granny's children were chalk and cheese, which did nothing to enlighten a six-year-old.

Just after my ninth birthday, my mother sat me down. 'Grandma is very unwell, so your father and I are going to see her and you are to stay with your Aunt Reda and Uncle Edward for one night.'

In my excitement I almost overlooked my concern for Granny.

'I'm going on the train to Grandma's,' continued Mother, 'and Father will come after taking you to your aunt. We'll fetch you tomorrow. I've packed your bag. You must remember your manners.'

'Of course she will,' said Father. 'Are we ready?'

'Give Granny my love,' I said when we dropped Mother at the station. 'Tell her I'll make a card at Aunt Reda's.'

As we left the station a worry struck me.

'Daddy, I forgot my crayons. Will Aunt Reda have some for Granny's card?'

'You needn't trouble yourself on that score,' he said. 'Remember, Aunt Reda will be upset because Grandma is her mother as well as mine and we're both worried that she's ill.'

'Doesn't she want to see Granny?'

'No, she's already visited and phoned me to say that Grandma wasn't well and wanted to see me. Grandma suggested you could visit your aunt. You'll be a good girl, I know.'

Standing now in front of Reda's paintings I recall the terraced house in Bury St Edmunds, very neat and rather gloomy. After saying hello to Uncle Edward, Aunt Reda took me to my room. We climbed one staircase and then a narrower one to the second floor. My room was south facing with sunlight spilling over a high, old-fashioned bed covered

40

with a puffy patchwork eiderdown. Opposite was Aunt Reda's studio. Cramped and chaotic, it was the most magical place I'd ever seen. An easel held a mysterious draped canvas. An old table hosted haphazard pots of brushes and palette knives. There were squeezed tubes of paint; smears of colour marking the table's surface. Straggly dead flowers in a vase dropped papery petals over books and pencils. A few drawings and pictures were displayed, but stacked together were more canvases, faces to the wall like naughty children. Best of all was the smell; linseed oil and turps. I breathed deeply and drank in the heady aroma.

Aunt Reda smiled. 'You like it?'

I pointed at the canvases. 'May I see them?'

'Help yourself. Rubbish from years ago, probably. I haven't been through them. One or two might be worth hanging on to.' She picked up a couple of brushes and smeared some paint on an old plate. She removed the cloth from the easel. All I could see was a few lines; it didn't look very interesting.

I looked through the stacked canvasses. Most were portraits of angry looking women in livid colours. I wasn't expecting such ugliness and felt overwhelmed with disappointment. I tried another stack and found, between two dark seascapes, drawings on thick, stiff, creamy paper. Some executed in pencil, some in charcoal and others in pen and ink, they were all of the same person; a young man with hair flopping over his left eye. Here he was eating an apple, here smoking a cigarette, here hunched in a chair and here sleeping, his arms thrown above his head, and lastly, lying naked on a bed. I had never seen a naked man apart from a few pictures of Michelangelo's David. My eyes were drawn to the unfamiliar.

I checked to see if Aunt Reda had noticed what I was looking at, feeling sure she would be angry if she knew what I'd found. She was intent on her work, her back towards me. I looked again at the drawing and found myself studying not his masculinity but his expression, in which I recognized vulnerability. I couldn't define it, but I knew that the young man was experiencing loss.

I carried on looking through the pictures. There were two of a woman with a baby, reminiscent of a Madonna and Child. The woman was sad and the baby faceless and unreal. Disregarding them I carried on to the bottom of the stack. Here was a painting on canvas stretched on a crude frame. I turned it over and immediately fell in love with it; a still life of a kitchen table with a blue checked cloth, a basket of eggs, a jug and two mugs. On the windowsill sprawled a marmalade cat and through the open window was the barest impression of an apple tree in blossom.

'It's Granny's kitchen!' I exclaimed with delight. 'It's exactly the same only a different cat. Mouser's black and white.'

Aunt Reda turned. 'Oh yes, I did it there. My Bonnard phase,' she said inexplicably and turned back to her work. 'Would you like it?'

'Do you mean to keep? For my very own?'

'Of course. Everyone should have a picture they love and every picture should have someone to love it. That cat was long before Mouser. He was called Coopers.'

'I'll draw a picture of this picture on Granny's Get Well card. I think she'd like that.'

I drew my card, faithfully copying the details in my aunt's painting, while Aunt Reda worked. Downstairs, Uncle Edward was making tea. While I munched toasted crumpets dripping with butter, Aunt Reda made a sketch of me in charcoal. I thought she might let me have that too but she didn't offer and not wishing to be greedy I didn't ask. The following morning Uncle Edward found sheets of brown paper for my still-life. He wrapped it carefully and tied it with string.

My delight at owning the painting was dimmed by my parents' reaction – my father muttered about Reda's daubs. I dozed as we drove home, hearing only a handful of their words as they talked softly. 'Must say, Edward's a decent enough chap. He's been a good influence.'

A few days later Father told me that my grandmother had died. Alone in my bedroom I unwrapped my picture and gazed at it remembering the warmth of Granny's kitchen. I wept knowing I would never see Granny again. I was also worried about Mouser. Mouser, I was told later, had been taken care of.

When I asked if I could hang the picture on my bedroom wall, my father told me it would require special holes for which he didn't have the right tools. I didn't persist but carefully re-wrapped it in the sheets of paper, stuck them down with tape and placed it under my bed.

I hoped there would be another visit to Aunt Reda but when I asked, was told that there would not, for reasons I was too young to understand. Soon after, on a warm April day, when my mother did her annual spring-cleaning blitz, I discovered my picture had disappeared. I tore down to the dustbin and there it lay by the bin. Devastated by my mother's treachery and the near loss of my treasure, I retrieved it and slid it behind my wardrobe, too heavy for my mother to move in her next spring-clean. It lay there untouched and waited for me to grow up.

When Aunt Reda died my mother did not accompany my father to her funeral.

I left home for university and my picture came with me. I spent a good deal of my precious grant having it professionally framed.

'A Reda Martin,' said the framer admiringly. 'Worth something. Her Bonnard period. Her work's becoming quite sought after, quite valuable.'

Little did he know just how valuable it would become. To fill the gap in my ignorance, I spent the rest of my week's money on a book about Bonnard.

Aunt Reda's painting has been my constant companion and for fifty years we have not been parted until I was asked to loan it for this exhibition. Its presence consoled me when my father died and soon after when my mother joined him. Sorting through her papers I discovered answers to my questions that had been avoided in childhood. I learned her secrets and sought solace from the picture's familiarity.

After her funeral I made my way, once more, to the gloomy little house in Bury St Edmunds. A woman wearing an overall opened the door.

'You'll be Mr Edward's niece,' she greeted me taking my damp coat. 'He's in his study. I'll bring tea.'

His study was as I remembered, with the old polished desk on which lay three pens in a neat row next to a pile of accountancy books. I doubted the books had been opened for many years.

I was shocked by how old Uncle Edward had become. He looked at me wordlessly and beckoned me to a seat by his chair near the welcoming fire. As I bent to kiss his cheek, he grasped my hand.

'My dear, you are a breath of life. I always hoped you would come. I miss her every day and you are so like her.'

Edward handed me a parcel wrapped in brown paper and string. Inside lay a book; *A Life in Pictures* by Edward Martin. On the cover was the same photo that now adorns the glossy brochure.

'It's all here for you, my dear,' he said. 'I forget so much now, but it's all in here. There's a sketch for you too.'

I learned about Reda's life through the pages of her husband's privately published book. I'd known about her wartime childhood and the loss of her father in 1944, but the stormy years of her teen-hood, her home-leaving to live in an artists' commune were new, as was her brother's disapproval about her illegitimate child, given away with anguish. I learned of her refuge in marriage to Edward.

Her life was also documented by her own work in colour reproductions alongside works of the artists who were her inspiration. There was a still life, similar in style to my heirloom, alongside one of Bonnard's. I recognised it from my book.

I look around the gallery at Reda's work, mostly unknown pieces but some familiar. I recognise paintings of the angry woman. I see the mother and faceless child, the drawings of the young man, the very ones I studied as a nine-year-old. I understand his expression now. He was about to lose Reda and his unborn child. I have seen that expression reflected in my mirror when mourning for the losses in my life.

'Wonderful work,' gushes a woman. 'Especially the drawings. The one of the child...' I follow her gaze to a charcoal of a nine-year-old girl eating buttered crumpets. It is Reda's only titled piece: 'My daughter.'

SILKEN THREADS

Helen de Búrca.

@helenlechat

A giantess, Neringa, created this bank of sand – so the story goes – to hide her lover from a dragon. It is an ephemeral place, a clustering of bark and dust, wavelets and opalescent skies; the materials Neringa had to work with, although beautiful, were sparse. Tree roots have bound it together for only a couple of centuries; opaque water the colour of malachite nags at the land, reminding it continually that the ragged golden fringe marking its edges is disputable.

At this moment, were Neringa in my place, she might have left him to the dragon.

It's totalitarianism, he says, his eyes stones in an anger-stiffened face. We're outside. It's the open air. If I want to smoke a cigarette, it's my own business. I can't believe she did that.

I adjust my position in such a way as to continue appearing attentive while removing myself as far as possible from the circle of indignation that surrounds him. As I do so, I catch sight of a tiny, neatly formed spider with a fat round body and graceful industrious legs. The nearby lagoon offers perfect incubation conditions for mosquitos; consequently, there are well-nourished spiders everywhere. This one has cleverly woven her web across the mouth of the old-fashioned lampshade above our heads.

What's she doing bringing two children here anyway, he says. People come to bars to smoke and drink, that's what bars are for.

The mosquitoes, stupefied or bedazzled by the light bulb, seem not to recognise their trussed-up fellows, bound in silk but unmistakable. I wonder whether spiders find them as annoying as humans do, or whether the hunting instinct obliterates everything else. Up and down they dart, whining, tipping the threads of the web with all the presumed invulnerability of bullies throwing stones at a chained-up dog. I watch tensely, willing one of them to be caught out by its own mischief.

If she doesn't want her kids being near smoke, she shouldn't bring them to bars, he says. And seriously, who makes a gesture like that to a total stranger?

I don't point out the obvious: that we share no common language with the woman except that of the most brusque and obvious of gestures. I am still listening to him, but my eyes are riveted to the web: a mosquito has at last brushed by it a little too rudely, paused for a moment too long, and the spider is upon it. The speed of its reaction is astounding. Almost immediately, the mosquito is paralysed.

Such dexterity, such an admirable ability to measure, react, seize. And, even more than that: such patience, such an admirable capacity to wait for the right moment.

He has been talking in this furious undertone for at least fifteen minutes now, his eyes fixed on the woman who is blatantly ignoring us. She guides a straw into an infantile mouth with the same hand that, earlier, made the violent and almost obscene gesture that provoked this fit of anger and – am beginning to realise – of hurt.

However, his voice is beginning to change slightly, the tone of it indicating that his mood has been shifting almost in parallel to my own. The possibility is approaching that soon we will be able to go back to discussing what we will do tomorrow, on the last day of our scanty holidays. Circling our heads now is the right moment, the one that will open up all the others.

Very soon now, I will catch it, that moment. When I do, I will ask him to describe to me again how, when we were cycling in the forest earlier today and when he stopped to check that I had not fallen too far behind, he had seen a fawn bounding away.

I watch the little spider as, her prey neatly wrapped, she retreats to a corner of her web. Her front legs begin to weave with calm dexterity, repairing the threads that were torn when the mosquito blundered into them. Soon, the web is whole again.

I wait until the torrent of words slows, halts, reverses its tide. Then, as if I barely notice what I am doing, I turn my chair back towards him.

THE JAR OF IDEAS

Marcia Woolf

www.marciawoolf.com

I was still young, three or four years old, when I was first left in the care of my Grandmother for the day. Lotte was my mother's mother: a towering, angular, pale woman with sleek grey hair and eyes the colour of water in sunlight. I was fascinated by her: she was strangely vague and distracted, and it seemed to me, even then, that Lotte was not really aware of my presence in the house. I followed her, asking questions, as small children do, always mindful that she might stumble over me, so far was I below her line of sight. From time to time Grandmother would stop what she was doing, scan the horizon, eventually locate me in the room and then give a short, soft sigh: not a wistful exhalation, but a faint expression of impatience tinged with what I now recognise as disappointment. Her answer to my many questions seemed always to be "perhaps".

She didn't tell me not to do things, unlike those adults whose eyes would follow an unfamiliar child around anxiously, anticipating inconvenience, checking for damage and dirt. Lotte merely left me to my own devices. It was a miracle that I came to no harm in her charge: as an adult and a parent now myself I shudder at her haphazard approach, her unaccountable freedom from obligation, her overweening sense of self. I was seemingly insignificant to her. Meals came at irregular hours: foreign food, designed for adults wielding cutlery with expertise. She paid no attention if I used finger and thumb; made no attempt to teach either table manners or dexterity with eating irons. But I could watch her if I wanted, and I did. I learnt. I observed as she combed her lustrous silver mane; as she applied a veneer of lipstick, the colour of winter holly berries; as she rolled her long pale stockings onto her long white legs, snapping the suspenders shut. I looked on as she inspected her face in the mirror, turning this way and that, frowning. I could see when her neighbour came to call; watched as my Grandmother slipped hastily behind the larder door, silent as a shadow lengthens in the dusk, ignoring his tap-tap for as long as it took for him to tire and leave, taking his flowers with him. I noticed when she climbed the uneven stairs to the attic room, clicking the ancient latch behind her, but it was a long time later, when I found the notebooks and discovered what she had been doing there, alone, that I really saw my Grandmother. It was then that I opened her bureau drawer, cautiously, feeling the runner creak along its unaccustomed rail, and recognised with almost disbelief her name on the faded, fraying jacket of a book: and under it another, and another still, and some translated into other languages. And there were sheaves of paper, bound with rotting bands, strewn over with her fine, urgent, hypnotising script. But as a child, I watched as she wound the striking clock, and returned it to the dead centre of the mantelpiece, setting its ormolu feet precisely back into the footprints it had made in a powdery layer of dust, running her finger regretfully over the damaged corner of its case, remembering. I saw that she smoothed the bedlinen with her long veiny hand, and snipped at the dying flowerheads with vicious secateurs; handles worn, but blades still sharp as glass. Yet I came to no harm.

One day, in my first autumn holiday from school, I was listlessly trailing Grandmother Lotte around her faded old house when she suddenly turned to me.

"You must be bored. We shall find you something to do."

I looked up at her, wide-eyed, apprehensive at what she might have in mind.

"Come with me."

She beckoned. I followed her obediently, reluctantly, into the dining room, a dreary salon almost never used, filled with dark carved furniture and heavy Turkish rugs. Motes of dust glittered in the air as she strode ahead. There was a pungent, oppressive, atmosphere in that room; an odour of soot and sandalwood, at once familiar and exotic. Balanced precariously on the hideous ornate sideboard there was a porcelain figurine, a woman draped in flowing robes, fancy beyond all imagining, one leg extended, her arms outstretched in a balletic pose, a tiny gold crown perched on her aristocratic head. The ornament was too close to the edge: even as a child, I could see it was poised to fall, as if the dancer had it in her mind to jump. Lotte passed it by, her sleeve nearly sending the poor fragile thing to her death, but the dancer teetered on the brink and regained her composure, Lotte oblivious. "Here," she said. "You see this pot?"

On a small mahogany table in a corner of the room stood the squat Oriental jar, octagonal, fitted with a neat lid. It was predominantly blue and white, with touches of red, green and orange highlighting its intricate surface pattern of scrolls. I approached it warily.

"Don't be afraid."

I studied her face for clues.

"This," she announced, with a flourish of her hand, "is the Jar of Ideas."

She laughed at my startled expression.

"How can a jar have ideas?"

Lotte gave me an enigmatic smile. Delicately, she removed the lid and set it aside. Then, holding back her sleeve with one hand, she extended the other delicately into the jar, as if trying to find something in there. I held my breath. After a few seconds, she carefully withdrew her hand, its fingers closed. Now I was curious.

"What is it?"

"What do you think?"

"Is it treasure?"

Lotte's eyes widened. She smiled. She winked.

"Tell me Grandma. What is it?"

Still she kept her bony fingers tight around the mystery.

"Is it a chocolate? A krona? It must be something tiny..."

"No, it's something very big."

I giggled. "It can't be. What is it? Tell me!"

Slowly Grandma Lotte opened out her hand, and there, nestling in the palm, was nothing at all.

"That's silly. You've played a trick on me."

No doubt I pouted and made to turn away, but she stopped me.

"You can't see ideas, Ilse."

I looked more closely at the empty outstretched hand, as disillusion circled, scenting new blood.

"How do I know it's there?"

Grandma Lotte smiled again. "It's not there. It's here." She tapped her head. "It's flown into my mind. That's where ideas live. They can't exist freely, by themselves in the open air: they need to keep warm and be fed and grow big and strong, before they can do their work in the world."

I was staring at her now, wondering if she was one of the mad old ladies who populated my storybooks. Maybe she was going to sprout fangs and big hairy ears and eat me up. She pointed gleefully, mischievously, at the jar.

"Do you want to try?"

"No."

"It won't harm you. See: just put your hand inside, and when your hand comes out an idea will come with it and find a home in your head."

"I don't want an idea in my head."

Lotte laughed. I suppose the grown-up me would have laughed too. She took hold of my hand.

"So put your fingers into the jar, and find out what's inside."

"I don't want to!"

She was gripping me tighter now, determined that I should play her game, but, alarmed, I resisted and wriggled my hand free from hers.

"What's wrong? Ideas can't hurt you Ilse."

I hesitated.

"How do the ideas get out of your head?"

My Grandmother was prepared for that question. She nodded, sagely, as if by answering this all possible objections might be overcome. As if she understood my trepidation; had once asked the very same thing herself. She bent towards me, and whispered.

"When they are big enough, and ready to come into the world, then you can write them down, that's how they escape. Or, you open your mouth – and out they pop!"

As she said this, she thrust her head and her wide parted lips towards me, sticking out her tongue and baring her teeth like the wicked old witches in my stories. I shrieked, stumbled away, and struck my head against the sideboard.

When my mother arrived at six o'clock, she was concerned to see Lotte at the kitchen table, carefully arranging pieces of broken porcelain.

"Mother? What happened? Oh, no. The dancer. Not the dancer."

Then she saw me, quiet by the hearth, reading my book of fairy stories.

"Ilse? Was this your fault?"

Before I could speak, Grandma Lotte scraped her chair back and rose, so that she stood head and shoulders over my mother, who was, inexplicably, a tiny woman sprung from the loins of a giantess. Grandma's hand waved airily over the broken ceramic limbs, dainty shards of gilded coronet and scarlet robe.

"Don't blame the girl Grethe. We were playing. It was an accident."

I shot my Grandmother an accusing look, which Mother detected immediately. She spoke to Lotte in a tone I'd never heard her use before; quiet, but hard and angry.

"Did you frighten her?"

Grandmother peered down at her daughter over half-moon glasses.

"Whatever makes you say that?"

Mother pursed her lips. I sensed it was time to go home, and slid down from my chair. I didn't know it then, but she would be lying in her coffin before I saw my Grandmother again.

Mother and I went to the back door and she ushered me out into the chill evening air. It was dark, and the darkness smelt of fox. Underneath our feet the frost crackled and sparkled, platinum-white, like magical dust dropped from the moon. As we walked, Mother held my hand tightly and asked me what we had been doing all day. I was sure she was upset about the ornament. Because I felt she was annoyed with me, I talked to her instead about the Jar of Ideas. My mother listened in silence. I told her about Grandma Lotte sticking out her tongue and baring her teeth, and she laughed, but not as if she thought it was funny. I think she had heard the story before.

"So," she said, as we approached our own cosy little house, where the curtains were drawn and the lamps were lit. A thin skein of grey spiralled into the charcoal sky, and the sour odour of woodsmoke filled the air. Father was home at last. There would be a stew of venison and dumplings. Soon it would be Christmas, and I felt a child's tingle of excitement at the knowledge of it. A few transparent flakes of snow drifted tentatively earthwards, pioneers for the many that would follow before the night ended; the soft downy blanket that would suffocate every whispered endearment, muffle every footstep, stifle every snapping twig, all silenced, save for the mournful cries of wolves as they stalked the ridge, never finding solace, invisible under God's majestic canopy of stars. Mother paused as she turned her key in the lock.

"Did you put your hand into this Jar of Ideas?"

I thought I had done wrong; that Mother would be disappointed in me for betraying her in some way. I shook my head. Smiling, she stroked my hair.

"Good," she said. "We don't want Grandmother filling your mind with her nonsense."

The next day, and the days following, I stayed at our neighbour's house while Mother was at work. I sat at old Inge's scrubbed table in her whitewashed kitchen, drawing pictures of the wandering elk and spires of pine trees clad in pristine snow. And it was then that I began to write: stories about silver sprites who lived in the forest, and transformed themselves into icicles when the hunters came; and I knew, but told no-one, about the beautiful, wonderful, astonishing ideas growing in my head.

THE RIGHT THING TO DO

Susmita Bhattacharya

@SusmItatweets

I hand the cup to Mrs Dalal. As usual, she is crying, caressing her bruised arm. She barely looks up at me, but takes a deep sip of the tea. My Bhabhi tilts her head slightly, indicating me to leave. I return to the kitchen, worrying about the rice that needs to be cooked before the children come home from school. Then there's the fish to be cleaned and fried. And Sir's shirt needs to be ironed for tomorrow. Why does Mrs Dalal turn up with her bruises at the most inconvenient of times?

Mr Dalal is a respectable man, a teacher in a primary school. He goes to work on his blue Bajaj scooter, wearing the same coloured safari suit every day of the week. His moustache proudly displayed and his shoes always reflecting the sun. He hits his wife regularly. We all know that. But they are a respectable family, so we pretend we don't know that. And Mrs. Dalal? She comes sobbing to my mistress, my Bhabhi, each time showing off her bruises, showering abuses at her husband, and plotting to report him to the police. And after two cups of chai and biscuits, or on a lucky day, samosas, Mrs Dalal returns home, sated and at peace with the world again. Only to come back another day for the whole cycle to start again.

My Bhabhi is the queen of her castle. Sir treats her with a lot of respect. He is never angry when she goes shopping. She sometimes spends more than my monthly salary on just one sari (I have seen the receipts). But I don't mind, I also get big bonuses, not kicks and slaps like the maidservant across the landing from us. Sir is kind and he looks into my eyes when he talks to me. He asks if my money has reached my mother safely. I wonder why Mrs Dalal is Bhabhi's good friend. Why does she like to listen to her miserable stories? She needs to spend her time with some better people.

It's raining today. I see Mr Dalal in his black rubber raincoat, sloshing towards his scooter. The black clouds are hanging above the trees in the colony. The gulmohurs have cast a red carpet of petals in the compound. The petals swirl up in the wind and settle on car bonnets as though they have been offered in prayer to the cars. I don't want to go out on a day like this. I don't like the bottom of my salwar streaked with mud and rain, it takes ages of scrubbing to get it off. Mrs Dalal is hovering behind her curtains. I know she's waiting for him to ride out so she can come running here. I'm sure she has smelled the mutton kebabs I'm frying. Dolly has requested them for her after school snacks. Bhabhi lounges in the front room, reading her Filmfare magazine.

The doorbell's just gone. When I open the door, I stare. This time he's gone too far. Even with the handkerchief covering her eye, I know a black eye when I see one. My mother had plenty in her time. Bhabhi swears out loud, and then pulls Mrs Dalal into the living room by her hand.

"This is too much, she mutters. Why do you put up with it, Freni? The man is the devil incarnate."

I hover around, pretending to straighten the cushions, switch on the fan. I want to know.

"He is the devil," Mrs Dalal sobs. "But what can I do? If I leave him, where will I go? What will happen to my Kaevoo, maro baccha?"

I know that feeling. I know that excuse. I heard the same words from my mother's lips for years and years, before I ran away. I know that feeling of being helpless. And Mrs Dalal, respectable or not, is a helpless, pathetic woman.

I give her two helpings of kebabs and extra sugar in her tea. Her eye throbs purple and red, while she recounts the latest episode of Mr Dalal's tempers. I realise that even though Bhabhi listens to her ever so intently, she has never once shared her friend's trauma with her own husband. She never let Mrs Dalal's sad life cast a shadow on their relationship. I am grateful for that. I'm happy that Bhabhi has a husband who respects and protects her. She is lucky.

"Arjun's coming," Bhabhi shouts from the bedroom. She disconnects the phone and rushes into the kitchen, and starts to rummage through the fridge. I stand back, watching possessively. The fridge is mine. She hardly ever opens it. And when she does, she puts everything back in the wrong place. She chucks out the mutton curry I made last night. And the chicken nuggets. "Finish these by tomorrow," she says. "Arjun's coming. He's vegetarian."

I am just as enthralled by her stories of Arjun as the children are. They call him Arjun Mama, uncle. He is her cousin. And more importantly, he is an entemo – well, he studies insects. He does important research, Bhabhi says, on insects. She looks at her computer and says words like Milkweed Longhorn and Black Vine Weevil. What's so exciting about insects, I ask and she gives me a look.

"He's a very important man. Make sure he is comfortable here."

I nod and go off. A man who studies insects is of no use to me. I have seen enough insects in my village, I could teach him a few names here and there. How to treat a scorpion bite? Now that's useful. Beetles are a waste of time.

Arjun Mama is here. He is anything but a Mama. He's like a film star. Long hair tied in a ponytail, smart beard, eyes that are laughing all the time. The children love him. He is very good with tongue-twisters and riddles. Dolly can't have enough of him. He is here for two weeks. Doing some research nearby at the National Park. With all the rubbish dumped in the so-called park, he's sure to find lots of insects. Ants and cockroaches mainly. What a job, I think, glad to be doing the cooking and cleaning for one house only.

He is Bhabhi's cousin. Her mother's sister's son. They grew up together in Nagpur. She has very fond memories of their childhood. There's a certain light in her eyes when she talks about those days. It's always, remember we did this, remember we went there. Sir listens politely, but I can see he's feeling left out. Arjun never stays in the room alone with him. He always gives a big loud laugh and runs to find the children. With Bhabhi chasing after him.

Even Mrs Dalal is not entertained this week. I send her back yet again with her bruised arm yellowing and her anger mounting.

"Tell your mistress to give me a ring when she has a minute of free time," she sniffs and strides off.

I shrug. Bhabhi has no free time now. She's busy tinkering with the 'apparatus' and 'log book'. She polishes the hand lens with her husband's chamois cloth. She's sorting the aerial nets and containers. They are going to find the Vindhyan Bob, she announces. A rare butterfly in Mumbai. In this concrete jungle, a rare butterfly exists, she giggles.

Arjun steps closer to her, and speaks. "Yes, right in front of me now."

I see her eyes flicker and then she turns away.

They return home, tired and spent. No butterflies in containers. But flushed faces and secret smiles. I stay in the kitchen, avoiding them. I don't want to hear their laughing voices. I can only worry for Sir. He doesn't know. He's at work, working hard for this family. But she? When Sir comes home, later than usual, Arjun has already gone to bed. He claims a headache coming on. Bhabhi sits with Sir while he eats. She tells him her afternoon adventures in the National Park. Her efforts at trying

60

to spot the butterfly. Her voice is too loud. Her voice is too bright. She is trying too hard to convince him. He listens politely, asking questions, scooping roti and aloo subzi into his mouth. I feel a burning anger. I want to cook him his mutton curry. How dare this Arjun man make Sir have to compromise?

The days go by quickly. Bhabhi's moods have changed. She is now quiet and thoughtful. She doesn't accompany Arjun to the forests. He too seems subdued. He is all business now, typing into the laptop, no tongue-twisters or jokes. I can feel Sir's impatience as well. I see that he avoids their company.

She finally lets Mrs Dalal in and listens to her complaints with rapt attention. Maybe this ritual helps her believe in her marriage. The terrible deeds of Mr Dalal helps her to hold on to her husband and appreciate him. While they toy with their biscuits and tea, Arjun announces he's going on his last hunt for the Vindhyan Bob. Would she like to come? Bhabhi hesitates, glancing at Mrs Dalal. Then she shakes her head. No, she says.

"I need someone to carry my apparatus." He is pointing towards me.

"I would love to go," I say. "I've never been to the National Park."

They exchange looks. Mrs Dalal's eyes are popping with curiosity. I can see she is quite taken in by Arjun's good looks. She smiles at him, her hands trying to cover the purple bruise on her arm.

As we get out of the lift, struggling with the apparatus, we hear a clatter of footsteps coming down the stairs.

"Wait," Bhabhi pants. "I'll come too. I managed to get rid of her."

I watch them together. They try hard to look disinterested. But I know a thing or two about body language. We struggle through the undergrowth, looking for this butterfly. Vindhyan Bob. What a name for a butterfly. I want to keep pace with them, but I keep getting distracted by everything around me. It is quiet here. Surprising as it is so close to the highway. I can see the tops of apartment blocks in the distance, above the trees. I can hear the din of the traffic. I look angrily at Arjun. If my Bhabhi's marriage is to break, it would all be his fault. Everything right now is his fault. I wish we never find this butterfly. That will serve him right.

She gives a yell, and we rush to her.

"Is this it?" she asks eagerly. It is the most ordinary of butterflies. Brown, speckled. No glorious patterns or colours. No drama. Just a normal little butterfly.

"This?" I say, losing interest.

"Yes, this!" He whoops as he drops his net onto the butterfly.

"Are you going to kill it?" Bhabhi asks. "Don't, please don't."

He glances at her, and shakes his head. "I'm afraid I have to preserve it. Document it."

Bhabhi looks away. Her lips are trembling. "I didn't come here to kill the rare butterfly," she says. "Can't you take a photo? Let it enjoy its freedom."

But he has already snared it, and closed the lid on the jar. The butterfly flutters, crashing into the glass walls.

"Let's go," he says.

We stumble back to the car. This time, Bhabhi sits in the back with me. On the front seat, the Vindhyan Bob keeps fluttering for dear life.

Back home, I rush to do my chores as usual. At the end of the day, I go to the bathroom to soak the dirty clothes in the bucket. That's when I look at the mug of toothbrushes by the sink. All these days, Arjun's red toothbrush has leaned shamelessly against Bhabhi's. But today, she has removed it and placed it in another tumbler by the window. I push the red toothbrush further away and grimace. It is the right thing to do.

THE RYCHENKOV RUBY

Mandy Huggins

@troutiemcfish

My father strode into the bedroom, preceded by a rush of cool air from the gallery. He walked over to my mother at the dressing table and rested his hands on her shoulders for a moment as their eyes met in the mirror.

'Don't be long darling, the car will be outside in ten minutes.'

He ruffled my hair on his way out, and my scalp tingled at the touch of his fingers. He eyed my mother's pearls as I fastened them around my neck.

'Very glamorous, poppet. Don't vex Nanny P whilst we're out, and don't go to sleep too late. No reading until midnight.'

I nodded and smiled, inhaling his familiar sandalwood scent without taking my eyes off my mother as she swept her hair into a tortoiseshell clip. This was my favourite time, when I would sit cross-legged on the bed to watch her get ready. Her cream leather jewellery box was open in front of me, and I ran my fingers over the glittering tangle of diamante bracelets, necklaces of iridescent shells, and cocktail rings set with amethysts, topaz, and amber.

I looked up as she opened the wooden box on her dressing table. She took out the silver key and unlocked her drawer, lifting out the velvet pouch that contained her diamond earrings. Somewhere in that drawer was a worn snakeskin ring box that held the Rychenkov ruby, the ring she had inherited from her grandmother. It was set with the most beautiful deep pink stone, and was so small that it didn't even fit my mother's little finger. She had let me try it on once and it only just fit mine. I had begged her to let me keep it, but she refused. The ring meant too much to her and she was scared I would lose it. Her grandmother had hidden it when they'd escaped from Russia, sewn into the lining of her shoe with silk thread she had unravelled from her fraying scarf. I took it one day and buried it in my sock drawer, but the next morning it had gone, returned to its rightful place without anything being mentioned.

I never dared ask to see it again, but contented myself with the never-ending treasures of my mother's costume jewellery. That evening I tried on the daisy clip earrings that always pinched my ears, and the ivory bracelets that slipped off my lathe-thin wrists, before re-examining each of her evening bags, stroking the soft chiffon pleats and the oyster silk linings, opening and closing the tiny jewelled clasps. There was always the hope of finding a leftover treasure inside; a lawn handkerchief stained with a lipstick kiss, or a ticket stub from the opera.

Then my mother asked the usual question.

'Which is it to be, darling?'

I handed her the blue velvet bag, and held my breath as she twirled it in front of the mirror before dangling it from her wrist by its slender chain.

'Good choice, sweetheart. Don't forget to make yourself some supper. And like your father said, don't annoy Nanny P, it's her night off. You can stay up until ten seeing as it's Saturday.'

I woke up later to hear voices in the hallway below. My parents were back early because my mother was feeling faint again. Crouched against the banisters, I watched my father carry her into the house, her bag still tangled around her wrist. I noticed straight away that it wasn't the blue velvet, but the turquoise silk.

My mother had betrayed me.

When I cried, Daddy put his arms round me, assuring me that she would be well again before we knew it. He wasn't aware that she had betrayed me, or of everything that was thrown open to question. How many times had she swapped her bag? Once? Three times? Had she ever taken the bag I had chosen for her?

The following Saturday my mother went out to lunch with her friend, Daisy Darlington. As soon as she left I slipped into her room and took the silver key from the wooden box. My hand trembled as I opened the drawer. The velvet pouches containing her diamond necklace and earrings were at the front, and at first I thought the snakeskin box was missing. But it was there, tucked away at the back underneath a small bundle of letters. I opened it to make sure. The ruby was as beautiful as I remembered. I tucked it in my pocket and re-locked the drawer, carefully replacing the key under the hair grips and ribbons in the chest.

I walked downstairs and out into the garden, holding the box tightly inside my pocket. Nanny P had heard my footsteps in the back hallway and called out after me.

'Don't be long, Margaret! Your lunch will be ready in half an hour.'

I crossed the lawn and went through the door into the walled garden, then sat on my favourite bench under the honeysuckle arbour. I took out the box and slipped the ring onto my little finger, but in the sunlight the ruby looked over-bright and garish, like a cheap paste stone from Woolworths. There was to be no joy in my chosen revenge after all, just a vague feeling of loss and a sudden revulsion at the cloying scent of the honeysuckle. I stood up and ran out of the garden, across to the five-bar gate, and through the long dry grass to the centre of the meadow. Then I slipped the ruby off my finger and threw it as hard as I could into the tangle of grass and willowherb. When I returned to the house, I replaced the empty box at the back of the drawer.

My parents went out for dinner as usual that night, but I didn't go up to my mother's bedroom to watch her get ready. In fact I didn't go again for some time. Instead, I sat with Nanny P in the kitchen, drinking her special cinnamon coffee and watching crime dramas on the portable television. I only ever went upstairs after I'd heard the front door bang shut and the crunch of tyres on the gravel.

Nothing was said about the Rychenkov ruby. Sometimes I was sure my mother was going to mention it. She would come into my room without knocking, her face stern, and my heart would quicken. But it would always be about something else.

Part of me was disappointed. Either she hadn't noticed the ring was missing, or she didn't care. Whichever was the case, it went to prove that the ruby hadn't been precious after all. It was another betrayal; another lie.

I went back to the meadow once and tried to find it, but the grass was too long. I half-thought I'd look again after it died back in the autumn, but a few days later I saw John, Nanny P's brother, crouched in the field with his metal detector, digging close to where the ring would have landed.

The following Saturday I decided to go up to my mother's room whilst she was getting ready to go out, just as before.

She was so happy to see me that for a moment I felt guilty. As usual, she asked me to pick an evening bag, and after a moment's indecision I handed her the champagne silk. She slipped the chain over her wrist and admired her own reflection in the full length mirror, then turned on her heel as if to leave. As she passed the dressing table she paused for a moment before taking the silver key from the chest. She unlocked the drawer, took out the snakeskin box and handed it to me.

'You can try on the Rychenkov ruby tonight, my poppet. Go on, open it.'

My hand shook as I opened the box, but my mother's face didn't alter. I looked down at it in shame, and then in confusion. The ruby was there, back where it belonged, glowing brighter than before.

She swept past me, a mink stole thrown hurriedly around her shoulders, then paused for a moment when she reached the door.

'John found it - with that metal detector thing.'

So she'd known all along that I'd taken it.

She didn't look at me, but left the room before I could say another word. I sat on her pink silk eiderdown until the light faded and Nanny P called my name from the hallway. I stood up and opened the bottom drawer of the wardrobe, took out the blue velvet bag and held it up against the taffeta dress. I had to admit that it had been a poor choice. The colour was totally wrong.

HE GAVE ME THE MILKY WAY (DEEP FRIED)

Olivia Tuck

thewingsofgrasshoppers.wordpress.com

"The usual?"

Benjy smiled like butter sliding down warm tea brack.

"Yep," I said. As always, I looked at him from under Boots mascara. My pupils photographed his dimples. His cheekbones. His earring. His copper eyes.

I walked home past Campbell's Chippy for these pieces of him. Nobody knew I took the route that wound round Sandalwood Road. On the odd occasion that Mum got home earlier than me, I'd tell her how I'd dawdled on the way out of school whilst swapping Geography notes with Lucy, or how Mrs Meredith had wanted to talk to me about Nothing-Bad-just-coursework, or how I'd had to go back for my coat after leaving it in Maths.

"You're on." He unwrapped the Milky Way and rolled it roughly in the batter. He plunged it into the spitting oil. It's a wonder we didn't hear it scream. It stayed quiet even as he speared it, delivered it from the fat and shrouded it in paper.

"Here you go. On the house."

My stomach was the innards of those Flying Saucer sweets. Fizzing.

I looked back at him as I opened the door. The wind ran its clumsy fingers through my hair before letting it fall back into position around my shoulders.

He winked at me. "See ya."

There was a strange keening noise as I let myself into the house. The sound of a cat with its tail caught in the door. Or of secret woman-howling. The noise was choked back as I peered into the gloom of the hall.

"Mum? Are you okay?"

She was sitting by the phone with a pile of paperwork in her lap. Her glasses were off; she was holding them by an arm, the way she used to take my arm and drag me through Sainsbury's. Her jaw was wet.

"Fine, fine." She stood up, letting the papers landslide to the carpet. "Are you?"

"Yeah, of course." I went up to her and put my arms around her neck, my cheek against her soft jumper. "Is it Ofsted?"

(Mum was the Head down at the Catholic primary. She was more frightened of Ofsted than she was of Hell.)

A gush of laughter came out of her. "No, thank goodness." She kissed my temple roughly. "I'm just a bit tearful. Probably coming up for my time of the month."

"But you…"

"Ssh. Go and get changed and have a look at your homework. I'll get started on dinner."

"What are we having?"

"Cauliflower cheese."

"Oh." I headed upstairs, disappointed.

"Molly, love?"

I halted, facing her. I knew what she was going to ask by her not-so-fast tone.

"Why are you so late?"

Of course, I had an answer ready. "I went to the library."

"Oh?" Her sad face went candlelight-soft. She loved Young People who went to the library without being nagged. "Which book did you take out?"

Damn.

"Emma." I gulped. "Ya know – by Charlotte Bronte."

"I see. That's a good one."

*

"Hello, trouble."

The day was weird. The sky was weighted down with storminess and sunset fire breathed along the horizon. The heat of the chippy clashed with the icy air in the doorway. It made steam.

Benjy's dimples puckered like kisses as he started the Milky Way ritual. As he fried, he started on about Westdown Comp, how the kids smashed shoplifted beer bottles across the playground and posted fireworks through old people's letterboxes.

"It's pants," he muttered. He looked miserable. It made my blood whoosh for him even more. "Anyway. Where d'you go to school?"

"St Hilda's."

"The Catholic school?"

"Yeah."

"So you're religious?"

"Uh...yeah. Yes."

He spread his buttery smile across his face. "Does that mean you can't get with lads?"

A moth fluttered in my ribcage.

"Um...it's not like that," I hastened to tell him. "Not nowadays. My mum wouldn't mind me, uh, having a boyfriend. She says I can, ya know, go on the Pill. And stuff. When I need to. She says she'll make the doctor's appointment herself. We just won't tell my nana."

My knees shook. No. No. I could not believe I had mentioned the Pill in conversation with him – and not shut up immediately afterwards.

He chuckled. Thankfully. Just chuckled whilst I burned, and said, "Your mum sounds like she's got her head screwed on."

"She has – sometimes."

He passed the parcel of deep fried chocolate over the counter. His palms were greasy.

"What's your mum like?"

"She's just Mum. My," he stuttered. I could feel the syllables on his tongue, little-boy words that simultaneously wanted both to stay inside him and to be free. "My parents split up last year. Dad met this girl not much older than me, working down the pub. Mum didn't see it coming. Neither did I – it's not like they argued or anything. She was gutted, to say the least. This place is Dad's business. Mum doesn't want me working here, but me and my dad are like that." He crossed his fingers. "I can't just cut him out, can I?"

The fryer hissed. His face was a whitewashed wall; empty, barely there. To this day, I don't know why I talked about the Pill, nor do I really know why I said what I said next.

"I haven't got a dad."

It was true. It had virtually meant the apocalypse as far as my nana was concerned. She'd nearly collapsed when my mum told her she was having a baby. She always said Mum had thrown herself away. Mum was never married to my dad, and when she got pregnant, he left. I'd never met him. I didn't want to.

"Moll?"

"I'm sorry." I was sheepish. "You didn't want to know that."

He grinned. "You're even prettier when you blush."

We met every day. At weekends, I'd tell Mum I was going to Lucy's, that we'd be going to the library for more classics. He'd deep fry me a Milky Way and we'd talk about what might happen if gravity pulled sideways, or Oasis versus Blur. Once we shared a cone of chips. Took alternate mouthfuls from a can of apple Tango.

I drew closer every visit.

He travelled round and round the rapids inside my skull. He was there, like the squiggly things you notice on the back of your eyes when you look into the sky. He floated about in my nervous system. Under the mosquito buzz of the hairdryer. During mock exams. On the phone, listening to Lucy go on about some lad she was snogging. In church, when I took Holy Communion for the first time.

It all made me think of a story Nana had read to me when I was little, about a girl who'd become so besotted with a pair of red shoes that the saints frowned down at her, because she could do nothing but stare at her feet in the shoes. Then she couldn't stop dancing: not until she died.

It was frightening. I hadn't known what being in love meant.

We were at school, in Mass, praying, when I decided I'd tell Benjy how I felt. A ray coming through the stained glass touched my shoulder blade. I took this as a sign. That afternoon, I paced down Sandalwood Road, through the cigarette butts and crisp packet corpses. The sun was molten metal amongst cygnet feather clouds. It glared, as if to tell me to turn back, to be a good girl, to go home to Mum and help her with the dinner.

I wasn't about to let it tell me what to do.

I'd got into the habit of pausing and looking through the window, just to watch him in the mundanity of the chores his dad had him doing. To appreciate how lovely he was.

So lovely.

Something struck me in the chest. The foundations of me trembled. Cracked.

The space behind the counter was occupied. There was Benjy. His collar was skewwhiff, which made him all the sweeter.

He was with a girl. A girl with a body like Elizabeth Taylor. With skin like a Dairy Milk and Coke Float curls past her shoulder blades.

Lucy.

Her giggle vanished as he leaned in and kissed her.

There were not enough tears in the ocean.

Not enough.

"There, darling, there now." This time, I was the one making the keening noise. I'd come home in an undisguisable state and collapsed onto the sofa with Mum, letting her cuddle me close.

"I love him," I sobbed.

She smelled of Persil and talc. "I know, I know." She didn't try to tell me not to take it to heart, or that because I was young it didn't mean anything. She held me.

All the lies I'd told ganged up to attack.

"Mum?"

"Yes?"

"Those times I said I was with Lucy" – Her name stuck in my throat, as if I were a sword swallower and I'd tried to knock back something too cold and sharp – "And that I was going to the library...I was with him."

"Oh, I knew that, love."

I swallowed. Hard. Wiped my nose with my fist. "How?"

She pressed a tissue into the crawl space beneath my coiled fingers. "Because despite my hope springing eternal, you never end up in the library unless I march you there. And I know a fib from ten miles away. You think I didn't slip off to meet boys without telling my mother?" She snorted. "Oh, I came up with some colourful excuses."

I'd never wondered what she'd been like when she was fourteen and at school, doodling hearts on her diary. Neither had I wondered about her being eighteen and at teacher training college, going to parties; or wondered about her as a twenty-something, in bed with my dad. I thought I knew every section of her: her neat teacher's bob, her glasses, her silk scarves, her squidgy Malt Loaf body, her soft hands with the shiny nails she kept short, her gentle voice with its authoritative melody. But I didn't. Not quite.

"Did you love my dad?"

The words were wounds: bruise-like, swollen at the edges. I'd never asked her. Ever.

"Oh, yes." She sniffed. "I'd adored him since I was your age. But nobody was sympathetic when it ended. You know how Nana is about it. Granddad wasn't much different. I loved your father so much. It's hit me hard recently. For some reason; age, I don't know. And…I've never said this to you, but I feel awful that you don't have your dad. I know I've been a wet weekend."

Pictures of her crying in the hall flashed across my retinas. Now I'd started imagining, I couldn't stop. I saw her, pumpkin-bellied, watching him pack a suitcase. I heard Nana's ugly words: well-placed darts digging into her skin.

"I don't need him. I don't. Really. I'm sorry." Two fresh tears plinked onto my school tie.

"You don't need to be sorry. I'm all right, I promise. Don't cry. Listen." She looped a strand of hair behind my ear. "When I was very young, I promised I wouldn't be the mother who brought her child up on guilt. There's nothing to be ashamed of in loving someone. Nothing at all."

I squeezed both her hands. We heard the birds quieten as twilight gathered on the doorstep.

"It's Saturday tomorrow," I said eventually. "We could go into town."

"I'd like that." She gently peeled my fingers off hers. "Want to order a Chinese for dinner?"

"Ohmigod – yes!"

It was when I made for the phone to dial the takeaway place. She said, "Oh, and Moll?" She glowed. I had never seen her smile like it. It was a fallen star in a dell – far more beautiful than Benjy's smile had ever been.

"Emma is by Jane Austen. Not Charlotte Bronte."

TWENTY-SIX LITTLE BONES

Maggie Davies

@maggiedavieswr1

After

There are three girls down in the street, illuminated by the fake Victorian gas lamps. Arms entwined, they weave their way towards another nightclub and more mojitos. The blonde, in five-inch heels and a flame-coloured dress, its hem flirting around slender calves, could have been my double. Once upon a time.

'What were you looking at?' frowns Sara, as I snap down the blind. My sister is checking what I'm up to, on her way home from A&E. She's doing twelve-hour shifts, back-to-back, this week. No wonder the blue eyes that examine me look so weary.

'Nothing.' I say.

'You'd say, if you need help? Wouldn't you?' she says, measuring out words like capsules of tramadol.

I restrain a glare. Help. The forbidden word. There are plenty of things I need. Things I can't have any more. I shrug in the direction of the black plastic bin liners in the corner.

'You could take them to a charity shop.'

Sara gathers up the nearest sack, its neck like a giant pursed and disapproving mouth. She hefts its weight in one hand while the other reads the shape of its contents. Then struggles to compose her face.

'Oh, Katie,' she says.

'Just get rid of them!'

It's the pity I can't bear.

Before

'How many bones? In the human skeleton?'

I'm home for the weekend and we're cross-legged on Sara's bed. A skull on her bedside table appears to regard the revision exercise with a dismissive smirk. Not a real skull, of course. A plastic one, for medical students.

'Two-hundred-and-seventy at birth,' she says, reaching slender arms towards the ceiling in a yoga upper body stretch. My baby sister is naturally beautiful. Not just attractive, as I am when tarted-up. She's stunning. If she made an effort, men would drool at the sight of her, like Labradors at an open fridge door. When she's finally qualified, a real, live doctor, I worry about them letting her loose on vulnerable male patients. They'll all have cardiac arrests.

'But only two-hundred-and-six in the adult.' She bends from the waist, in a pose that will have an absurd name. Yoga isn't my scene. I gave up after the Downward Dog. 'Because by then some have fused together.'

'Okay, smart-arse. How many just in the foot?'

'Twenty-six.' She settles into a lotus position and dispenses a smug look. Maybe I'll bribe her to be my secret weapon at a pub quiz night. 'A pair represent a quarter of the bones in your body.'

'Sounds disproportionate.'

'Feet are workhorses. They cope with decades of hard use.' She glances at the strappy sandals that I kicked off earlier, discarded on her bedroom carpet. 'Always assuming people wear vaguely practical shoes.'

'You sound more like Mum every day.'

Shoes take me up where I belong. Doesn't every woman crave gorgeous footwear? The higher, the more uncomfortable, the better? I reckon Cinderella swooned over that glass slipper, though it must have been torture to wear. Not my swot of a sister, of course. But for every red-blooded female they're essential. The snazziest killer heels make me feel hotter, my legs longer. Make me stand taller. Help me spot someone worth hitting on at a party. The trick is to find a pair you can dance in all night long, without ending up crippled the next day.

And I have scores, all in their original boxes with a photo taped on the end for quick reference. A fortune's worth of foot candy. Manolo Blahnik and Christian Louboutin. Exquisite sandals and architectural platforms. Even a few designer ballet flats, which ought to please Sara, but apparently don't support my instep properly.

Alastair adored my feet. He loved to caress them bare, of course, pale against his purple silk sheets. He admired their elegant arches in skyscraper heels. But it was the thigh-high biker boots I'd bought that really turned him on.

Dark-eyed, dark-haired Alastair was a miscalculation from the start. An ex-public schoolboy with a bogus estuary accent and a weird job in IT that I never fully understood. I hooked up with him in the lift of the building where my marketing company is based. He had a mild coke habit, but didn't press me to join him. And he was fit. My friends were gratifyingly jealous and the sex was awesome, though I knew from the beginning I wasn't the love of his life. That was his motorbike. A horrendously expensive Ducati Streetfighter. Black and silver, with touches of blood-red paintwork. Riding pillion behind him, pressed against the rigid leather of his jacket, I could feel its power over him. The thrill of speed, of risk.

'When I picture you on the back of that thing, I shudder,' objected Mum, tugging at the umbilical cord despite me being twenty-nine years old.

'Your mother's right, darling.' said Dad, always ready with a scary statistic. 'You're thirty times more likely to be killed in a motorbike accident than in a car.'

After

The truck was only marginally over the glinting cats' eyes marking the centre of the road, and Alastair hadn't even done a line of coke that night. But it was a juggernaut, driven on a surface slick with rain. Alastair limped away with cracked ribs and a dislocated shoulder. A miracle, the doctors said. Born to be hanged, he muttered later, unable to meet my eye. Anyway, after a dozen visits to my bedside in intensive care, he melted away, like the hand-made chocolates he'd brought that ended up with the nurses.

'Bastard,' Sara said. But I could see it. See what looking at me did to him. The guilt. Because there wasn't enough love. Never had been, really.

He's an attractive man, my surgeon. Which makes it somehow hugely worse. That, and the look in his eyes. He should learn how to hide caring about what he's had to do to me.

'When can I go home?' I demand.

'Maybe in two weeks.' He looks at his clipboard. 'You've done incredibly well.'

81

'And walk again? With a ... foot?'

I refuse to leave this place in a wheelchair. I want at least to look normal.

He pauses, takes an almost imperceptible breath. He will have done this dozens of times. 'You have to be realistic, Kate. After losing a foot, post-operative recovery can take as much as a year. You must give it time.'

I stare out of the hospital window. There's a mass of scaffolding outside. A builder's skip. It looks like they're trying to shore up the external wall. A hard-hatted guy is strutting his stuff by shinning up a ladder like a spider monkey.

'I'm so sorry,' the surgeon says. 'Things like this can't be rushed.'

I slouch in the chair in my bedroom and make myself look. I'm screwed, aren't I? Ugly. Gross. What man will ever look at me again with desire? My stump itches. The prosthetic foot is like something from those old Monty Python programmes Dad loved to watch.

Well, I refuse to go back to Norfolk, to sleep in the single bed of my childhood. To be fussed over. I'll stay in London. It's easy to be anonymous here. I won't return to my old job, either, though they're offering promotion and an increased salary to tempt me back. I'll work from home. Sort out some kind of consultancy deal. Financially I can manage. The insurance will help. I'll be like one of those hermit crabs: safely tucked into my shell, with my putty-coloured, carbon fibre foot for company.

Sara drops her backpack on the carpet, drapes her jacket over the spare chair and starts dragging squealing hangers along the rail in my wardrobe. She throws skirts and dresses onto the bed in a whirl of textures and colour.

'We're going clubbing,' she says.

'Since when?'

'I'm not taking no for an answer, Kate. I getting my sister back.' She picks over the clothes with slender fingers, her nails unvarnished and clinically short. 'Plus I need a break from having sixty patients in need of care in A&E. With half-a-dozen more waiting in ambulances outside.'

She holds up a skinny dress in silver grey crepe. It's a Victoria Beckham. Expensive. 'I'll borrow this. I've always envied your clothes. Lucky we're the same size.'

She pushes and pulls me into silk stockings, a tight black sequin skirt and a skimpy top, her expression reminiscent of when she was little, dressing her dolls. Always looking to me for approval. Then she digs around in the top drawer of the bedside table and thrusts my make-up bag into my hands. She's the big sister now.

When I finally link arms with her in front of the mirror, face on and outfit smoothed down, I have to admit you wouldn't know I was a cripple.

I may have only one foot, but I've got a pair of shapely legs and a good body. My balance is sort-of okay if there's something handy to grab hold of. I refuse to have a stick and the crutches are pushed under the bed. In the flat I simply lurch from one piece of furniture to another. But in a club, a sister's arm might be just the thing to get me to a bar stool.

I'll humour her. I wouldn't mind a well-made vodka Martini. I imagine the tinkle of crushed ice falling into a tumbler. The sshush of Vermouth being poured over. The rattle of a silver spoon, stirring. The transfer to the chilled, long-stemmed glass. The tang of zest in my nostrils from that twist of lemon. Theatre for a party girl.

Sara rarely gets a proper evening out and in that dress she's like something from a fashion shoot. She naturally gets invitations from the guys at her hospital, but there's someone she's been seeing - an overworked and bespectacled GP from Deptford - and they don't get a look-in. Saturday night for Sara and Dr Dedicated is an impenetrable foreign film.

She's brought a pair of sensible courts in her backpack, the kind Mum swears by, but she'll get away with them. Everyone will be looking at her face.

'A sequinned skirt with scuffed trainers?' I say, looking down at myself. 'Really cool.' Then I laugh. I actually laugh. This is so crazy.

'Sit down and stick your feet out,' she orders, reaching again into the backpack.

I freeze as she pulls out my almost-forgotten patent kitten heels, the ones encrusted with fake diamonds. Last seen at the bottom of a bin bag. Then I take a deep breath, ease myself down into the chair, and do as I'm told. She's right. Having an artificial foot isn't such a big deal these days. I can still wear fancy shoes. Enjoy dressing up. There's more to me than missing twenty-six little bones.

'I kept them for you,' she says, grasping my carbon fibre toes in loving hands and guiding them into a shoe. 'They're safe in their boxes. I knew you'd wear at least some of them again.'

I breathe in the scent of my sister: clean hair, traces of the Coco Mademoiselle I gave her for Christmas; all that unconditional love. Two strong women, getting on with life. Bring it on.

PERFECTLY PRIME

Sherry Morris

@Uksherka

The day Elvis Presley died we were in the car coming home from a family vacation. It was a fairly typical 1970's car journey as we made the four-hour drive from one side of our flat, empty, rectangular state to the other. Thanks to my little brother, the Old Maid playing cards had flown out the window while we tried to keep cool in the August heat. I was left to amuse myself by giving him Indian leg burns, mixed with Chinese frog bites. When Mom had had enough of Joey's yelps and threatened us both with the beating of our lives, I watched sweat trickle down my arm and listened to Dad punch radio buttons, grumbling and swearing about the poor quality of music on offer as he searched for an Elvis tune.

The announcement came through just as Dad resigned himself to a Tom Jones song-- Elvis had been found dead at Graceland of a suspected heart attack. We listened wide-eyed and open-mouthed. There wasn't any of that other stuff at the beginning: the binging on pills and food, or jokes about how The King died on his throne. There was just shock that a god had been struck down. Almost everybody I knew was a fan. Dad said It didn't matter about Mom and Joey was too young to know. It was me who always went out to the garage with Dad, where we'd sing Elvis tunes and dance. Sometimes he'd wear his Elvis hair and put on a leather jacket. When he curled his lip and shook his hips, he was almost Jailhouse Rock Elvis—until he started to sing. Hearing the news, I wondered how he'd cope. We'd had relatives die and get no more than a shrug out of Dad. But this was different. This was Elvis.

When the news bulletin finished, Dad switched off the radio and pulled the car to the side of the road. No one spoke. Eventually my brother asked if there was something wrong with the car. Mom said there was something wrong with Dad. He got out and we watched him pace along the shoulder, his arms wrapped 'round himself. After a while, Mom pulled out an emery board and started filing her nails. She switched on the radio, to a station playing jazz, but switched it off when Dad came back to the car. For the first time ever we drove home in silence. No music. No bickering. No swearing. No Elvis.

From then on, Dad spent even more time out in the garage. He'd sit in his lawn chair and play his Elvis records, saying he preferred them to the radio and the speculation that had begun. He'd start with the early-years, cranking up 'Heartbreak Hotel' and end with his all-time favourite: 'If I can Dream'. It was tempting to hold my ears when Dad belted out the chorus, but instead I clapped. When they showed his funeral on TV, Dad wouldn't watch. Said he'd rather listen to Elvis living than see him laid out dead. Then he'd head off to the garage with a couple of 12-packs.

Like Elvis, Dad had this thing about numbers. He'd thumb through his dog-eared copy of Cheiro's Book of Numerology while singing the opening lines of 'Blue Suede Shoes.' He started telling me we were specially connected to Elvis.

'It's all those 7s, you see, Cilla,' he slurred.

When I said I didn't he said, 'Elvis passed on the 16th of August, 1977. That's two 7's straight off the bat.' He held up two fingers. They were thick as sausages.

'Then, look at the date: 16. Add 6 and 1—what do you get?'

'Seven!' I cried.

'Exact-o-mundo,' Dad replied. A third finger went up.

'Now look here, I'm 37 and you're 7, right?'

'Right,' I answered, pleased he remembered how old I was.

'That's five 7s in total,' he concluded, holding up his pinkie and his thumb, showing me all five fingers now, wriggling them and making me laugh.

'Now here's the thing,' he said. 'If you add our ages, 37 and 7 and subtract two you get 42—the age of Elvis.'

'Wow.' I said enjoying this impromptu math lesson.

'So you see,' Dad said, 'we are clearly connected to Elvis.'

'Holy-moly,' I said. I couldn't wait to tell all my friends.

'And here's the bonus—7's are super-duper lucky.' Dad smiled at me and dropped his voice. 'I should take you to Vegas. With all the Elvis luck we got, we'd clean up big at the casinos, live the high life and leave this all behind.' He jerked a sausage finger back towards the house. 'I might even be able to get a gig.'

He paused to reach for another can. I noticed his cheeks and nose were red. Probably from all the excitement. The thought of going to Vegas was thrilling. I could be Dad's backup singer. I knew all the words to all the songs Dad knew. We could go at weekends so I wouldn't miss school. It was going to be great, living the high life.

At other times, though, the high life seemed far away. 'Forty-two, just forty-two,' he'd mumble. 'Died in his prime.' He'd sit in his lawn chair in the garage and stare out the raised door into the street. 'In his prime,' he'd repeat while shaking his head. If I'd been more mathematically advanced, I could've pointed out we were the ones, at 7 and 37, who were prime, not Elvis at 42. But Dad wasn't around by the time I learned about prime numbers. And he wasn't really in his prime when he died. He was fat, medicated out of his mind, and miserable—Elvis I mean, not Dad.

Elvis Presley was born on January 8th, 1935. As the 8th approached, I realised we had an additional connection to him. I couldn't wait to tell Dad. But he was hard to catch these days. He was coming home later and later during the week and sometimes not at all at the weekends, though he said he slept in the garage and woke up early to run errands. When he was home he'd pick fights with Mom, asking why she didn't dance as well as their friend Sally. Then he'd head out to the garage and his fully-stocked fridge. He started listening to the radio again—but it wasn't music this time. It was an on-going story about a man who had adventures in outer space. I didn't really get it, but at least it gave me time with Dad. After one of the episodes, I told him I'd found another connection to Elvis. But he just looked at me all empty. I could tell he didn't know what I was talking about.

'The 7s, Dad,' I reminded him. 'And now there's 8s.' Then I talked him through it. How Elvis's birthday was the 8th, it was 1978, I'd be 8 this year. He'd turn 38. I held up my fingers just like he had, hoping he'd remember. I couldn't figure out a way to work in Elvis's age, so I used his year of birth instead: 1935, adding up 3 and 5, subtracting 1 from 9. I said we were even more connected and super-duper lucky than we imagined.

'It'll be just like you said, Dad, with Elvis luck and a high life,' I told him. 'It's always gonna be me, you and Elvis.'

He had the strangest expression on his face. He was looking at me, but he didn't seem to see me. Dad left us a few months after that. If he did go to Vegas, Mom never said. What she did say was, 'Good riddance.' Then Grandma moved in and a whole bunch of Barry Manilow records appeared. I found Dad's records out in the garage. He'd left them. And me.

I told myself the records were consolation. He knew I'd appreciate them. I did. Sort of. I played them and sang along, pretending I was dancing with Dad. But it wasn't the same.

For a long time after that I wasn't sure there was such a thing as Elvis luck and thought if I'd found more 7s and 8s, or was a better dancer, maybe Dad would've stuck around. Or at least asked me to come visit.

Then, one summer, when I was a teenager, I came across a radio program about a man who hitchhiked around the galaxy with an alien while writing a travel guide. Listening to it gave me the strangest feeling. I'd heard this somewhere before. I listened to all the episodes. Then read the books. Eventually I figured out where I'd heard it. It's what Dad had been listening to out in the garage: Douglas Adams's Hitchhiker's Guide to the Galaxy. I learned forty-two was the answer to the Ultimate Question of Life, the Universe, and Everything. When I heard that, things fell into place. Dad had gone off to explore his own answers to the questions prompted by Elvis's death. It hadn't had anything to do with me. This was between Dad and Elvis. And he wanted to do it while he was in his prime. I couldn't hold that against him.

It turns out there is such a thing as Elvis luck. My husband, Dave, takes me out dancing, does a very convincing 'Jailhouse Rock' and has great hair. Sometimes we even perform together—as Delvis and Priscilla. I don't just sing back up. Some of the songs we've changed to duets and on a few I take the lead. We do pretty alright—bookings are steady. Now maybe Dad should've stayed in touch, phoned up now and again, sent a postcard. Or a birthday card. But maybe it's better this way. Because this way I can imagine he's super-duper lucky in Las Vegas with Elvis—where they're both perfectly prime forever.

PREDATOR

Lucy Corkhill

www.lucycorkhill.com

I'm sitting on the man's leather sofa wearing my short shorts, legs crossed. The man's gone to get me a glass of squash and a biscuit. Back in a minute, he said. Clean shaven, dark hair, skinny. Not half as friendly as when we met in the chatroom.

We'd had a laugh then, chatted about our favourite TV shows and what we were doing at the weekend. After a while he'd asked, Wot U warin?

My nyty! I typed. Slepover w my m8s. U?

Long silence - three, maybe four minutes, and then, Got my pjays on – zzzzz!

The room I'm in is okay, but it's on the top floor of a grimy block of flats. I got a noseful of dirty bins and dogshit and all sorts coming up in the lift. Ping! at the top, and he was standing at the door to his flat in jeans and a grey t-shirt. Not old old, but old. Didn't look right at me when he said my name, probably embarrassed because he was all, my m8s r sooo borin and cant do my hmwrk ahhhh! in the chatroom.

I hovered in the doorway which made him look up and down the corridor and pull me in to the flat, his hot fingers handcuffed round my wrist. He brought me in here, to this room, and said in a polite way to take a seat and he'd get me a drink. What's your poison? he said, the kind of stupid thing my step-dad says. I gave him a look that said I don't drink, I'm a kid. And he said, I've got orange squash and biscuits.

I can hear him clonking about in the kitchen bit of the flat. I bet he bought the squash specially, probably from the Co-op I passed on the way here. Maybe the shop girl wondered why he was buying kiddy squash.

Definitely lives on his own, you can tell from the room. A brown leather sofa, sagging in the middle. Big flatscreen TV on the wall, the remotes on a black plastic coffee table beside my knee. Sticky rings on the table, a folded newspaper, an empty can of coke and an ashtray that looks like it's been nicked from a pub. Four – no, five – butts in the ashtray. I scan the room for the fags – over by the door there's a shelf with some shitty nicknacky bits, loose change, keys, and a pack of Malboro with a lighter. The leather peels away from the bare backs of my legs as I get up. I take a fag from the packet, light it and inhale, a nice hit in the back of my throat. I see that underneath the Malboro packet there's a condom in a wrapper. I place the fags back carefully. The man comes into the room carrying a mug of orange squash and a pack of Hobnobs.

Bit young to be smoking, he says.

I can't tell if he's annoyed that I took the fag without asking, or just nervous. He goes over to the coffee table and puts the mug and biscuits down. Didn't expect you to be so young, he says, looking me up and down.

Right, I say. Didn't expect you to be so old.

I'm not that old, he says.

Older than I thought, I say. Thought you were at school like me.

D'you mind? he says.

I shrug, take another pull on the fag.

He sits on the edge of the sofa, pats the seat beside him. Wanna watch a film with me? he asks.

Alright, I say. From where I am standing near the door I can hear someone's shoes squeaking down the corridor.

I've got Frozen, he says. We'd talked about films in the chatroom, he'd said he liked the same ones as me which seems stupid now. He lifts the remote and the big telly blurts into life.

I first watched this film at home: me, Mum, my little brother Sean, all wedged on our old sofa that smells of one too many times the dog's slept on it. Mum with her navy uniform on, asleep within fifteen minutes after a double shift at the supermarket. We didn't wake her. It'd been nice just to feel the warm of her next to us and hear the funny whistling of her breathing. Sean looked at me over the top of Mum's head and we both smiled. We had enough money to buy a couple of those bags of popcorn, so it must've been before Graham moved in.

The man is staring at me. Wanna come and sit down? he says. He's trying to keep his voice casual, like he doesn't care.

Nah, I say.

Go on, he says. Come and have a bit of your drink.

I shake my head.

Is it because it's in a mug? Cos I can wash up a glass if you like, he says.

Nah, I say.

I like your shorts, the man says.

The whole time I've been letting fag ash drop onto the grainy carpet, but now the fag's starting to burn my fingers and I need to put it out in the ashtray. As I walk towards him he says, Good girl. I have to block his view of the telly to put my fag out, and as I step back he grabs my arm. Sit down, he says, in a different voice. So I do. I can tell he isn't going to pretend to be gentle now, there's some that do, but the way he's twisting my skin tells me he isn't one of them.

The sofa lets out a sort of fart when I sit on it. My heart's banging around in my chest, but the fart noise still makes me laugh.

What's so fucking funny? the man says, pushing me back.

No more Mr Nice Guy.

First time had been one of the men came to my step-dad's burger van. He looked through the hatch at me. Graham around? he asked, and I knew straight away he wasn't asking because he wanted to see Graham. I can't remember what I said, but he took it as a reason to come round the side-door and tell me he had some sweets in his truck. And then, suddenly, Graham was back, swinging two plastic shopping bags from his fists. Alright Dave, he said to the man, and the man shuffled off back to his truck, baggy jeans hanging low on a hairy arse. I could've told Dave that my step-dad wouldn't give two shits whether I went off to his truck as long as I was back to serve the next customers, but he found out soon enough. When it came to some things, Graham could be generous to his friends.

Then there was my chemistry teacher, Mr Chatham. Lots of the girls liked him because he was young and jokey, but he made a special fuss over me. I never did the homework but he always gave me good grades, turned a blind eye when I copied in class. So I knew it was coming when he asked me to stay after the bell. He put his hand on the top of my leg, asked me if I wanted to come over his house for extra lessons. The mushroomy tips of his fingers massaged the back of my neck and opened the top buttons of my school shirt. I didn't move or say anything, but after that he started smiling at me in class as if we had some special secret. It wasn't long before someone mentioned it to the headteacher and I found myself on a chair outside Mrs Cole's office, waiting for her to finish talking to Mr Chatham. I pressed my head against the wall so I could just about hear what they were saying.

You know we have to take these complaints seriously, Oliver, Mrs Cole said. Your job could be on the line.

Of course I understand that, Mr Chatham said, but to be honest I'd be grateful if you could move her to a different class. I find the girl – how shall I put this – frankly, predatory.

A pause. Mrs Cole mumbled something that ended with the words: that family.

She managed to squeeze a lot into those two words: Mum's prison sentence, the drugs, my sister's death, Sean's problems. Obviously I didn't expect her to know about the times Mum and I cuddled up on the sofa and listened to music, or we all made a cake from a recipe, or looked at photos of my sister together. And to be fair those times were thin on the ground since Graham came on the scene, but still.

No point waiting for Mrs Cole to call me into her office, I could tell who was going to come out worse. I walked out of school, and I haven't gone back.

Thinking about Mr Chatham reminds me of what I've still got to do, and it gives me strength. I can hear the telly yodelling out the Frozen Heart song over the man grunting into my hair. His hot paws are grappling at the flies on my short shorts. I bring my head up under his jaw, sharp and sudden, and feel his teeth sink into the soft meat of his tongue. He lets out a dog's howl and falls back against the sofa, his hand up to his mouth and blood running through his fingers, and I take the opportunity to pound my knee down hard into his groin, lift out the blade I've got inside my jacket and ram it up under his ribcage. Practise makes perfect, and I've been practising. First time, I stabbed and stabbed until I was soaked in blood, but I'm swift, neat now. I wiggle the knife side to side and up to the left. Sean's knife – what you want a blade for? he asked, sat on my back while I did my nightly press-ups. Keep me safe, I'd said. And it has. It has kept me safe. Not just me; lots of girls are safer now.

The man is bleeding away into his sofa, blood gurgling in his throat, as I wash my hands and the knife in the kitchen. I leave the flat quietly, picking up my rucksack on the way out, and take the stairs to shake the tension out of my legs. It's surprisingly hot and bright outside, a sunny June Saturday. I run through the list in my head, ticking the men off one by one. Another one down, just one to go. After that, I'm out of here. Got a roll of notes from Graham's burger van in my rucksack, a little splattered with Graham's blood, and cash I've taken from wallets on my way.

My feet feel light and springy on the pavement, as if I'm flying. I walk briskly through the unfamiliar streets, having carefully memorised maps of my route, past people in summer clothes out shopping, or sunning themselves in street cafes. Poor pale Mum will be working a double shift, she won't find out about Graham until later. Shame we won't be able to celebrate together, but I'll be long gone. I'll send her money, course I will, when things are more settled.

The knife in its sheath is skin-warm, hidden against my chest.

Number 48, Meadow Drive. I hitch my shorts up a bit, run my fingers through my hair, then ring the doorbell.

His face is surprised but pleased when he opens the door.

Mr Chatham, I say. Can I come in?

X ON A CORNER SQUARE

Jenny Gaitskell

@JennyGaitskell

When Mum told me Grandma was moving in, she taught me how to play Scrabble. I didn't think it was much fun, having to make the words you could, rather than the words you liked. It was not that sort of a game, Mum said, it was not really a game at all.

When Grandma came, she turned me into a hologram. I was seen but not heard, not speaking until spoken to, so not speaking much at all. The sofa wasn't my launchpad any more, it was her planet. I was stuck in orbit, sitting on the floor, where fidgeting was not allowed, no matter how quiet it was. I learned the pattern of the carpet off-by-heart, made up new words for all the browns, hoping Mum would ask me.

Mum wasn't talking much, probably because her face had gone so stiff. After a few days, at bedtime, I broke hologram rules and asked her. She told me Grandma was dragging us back in time, but she didn't know and couldn't help it.

I should have realised that Grandma was a time traveller. Her expression was like old photographs, but her hair was such a bright orange it had to be from the future. Her glasses were not only octagonal, but showed her everything I was about to do wrong. Since she'd been around, teatime always seemed so much further away and bedtime so much closer. I wondered about the golden clock she'd brought with her, with its whirling globes, four tiny worlds trapped under a glass dome. When she said I'd never be a scientist, I thought she'd met me as a grown-up, but Mum told her that things have changed, now I can be whatever I like. The future changes all the time.

For example, before Grandma moved in, I expected to watch Star Trek every single night. Afterwards, I only expected to watch the news and documentaries about the sad parts of history. I predicted that Sunday would be the longest day, even though it was the wrong time of year. I tried to use up all the extra minutes, but it didn't take me nearly long enough to read all of my library books, join every single dot to dot, colour everything inside the lines, and search for all the missing words. The only thing to watch on television was my own reflection, until six o'clock. I didn't know that yawning was rude, or that one day a train would come out of my mouth, but Grandma did.

Mum sighed and Grandma asked her what she had to sigh about. For a moment, it was like we were all floating in the great airless void that is space. Then Mum took a deep breath and said it was time for Scrabble and asked me to fetch it from the chest.

Only special things were kept in there, things for parties and Christmas, or left behind by dead people. It smelled like liquorice. I brought the Scrabble to the coffee table. It was from the past, the green worn off at the corners, the name written on the inside of the lid was my Mum's, but in handwriting like mine, now. Grandma said I was too young, but Mum said I'd played before. Grandma said she'd keep score. Mum agreed that she always did.

The bag of tiles sounds like something broken, but the tiles are smooth with lovely rounded corners. Grandma told me not to look, Mum said I wasn't a cheat. I wanted the K5, which is the best letter, but I didn't get it, just a silly O1, and had to go last. Grandma told me not to pout and I didn't think I had been, or had been just about to either, and to make sure I didn't, I pinched my lips. She had a different frown for each of her letters and huffed as though the tiles were misbehaving, too. She stared at them for such a time that I wondered if she was changing them into letters from a future turn.

To avoid fidgeting, I concentrated on the pink star at the centre of the board, the galaxy of double score blue giant suns and triple score red supergiant suns. Grandma's tiles turned the heavens back into a board. Her first word was P3E1E1V4E1. Mum said it was perfect, but Grandma didn't seem pleased. Mum quickly put down D2E1A1D2L1Y4, and laughed a bit like she was coughing. My word was P3I1N1E1. I liked it because it left P3O1O1 on my rack and nobody knew but me. Grandma told me I should use my O1, but that would have ruined it. Mum said that Grandma meant the word O1P3I1N1E1 and that it meant telling innocent victims what you think and what they should do, all the time. Grandma said that rather than be spoon-fed sloppy definitions I should be taught to look words up in the dictionary. I was sent to get it.

Grandma and Mum took their turns without waiting for me, complicated words with consonants all squished together. Grandma took the dictionary from me without thanks, as if it had floated over to her. I didn't mind because I got the best letter and played one of my top one hundred best words ever, S1P3O1O1K5. They were only interested in the word Mum had played before it, S1T1Y4M3Y4. Spelling is important, everyone knows that, but Grandma and Mum were arguing about the morals of people who get it wrong, until Grandma slammed the dictionary shut, scribbled a number under each of our scores. Mum said she was betting her sanity on this game. She wiggled her eyebrows at Grandma like she was daring her.

There are a hundred tiles in Scrabble but it felt like a septillion. I played one or two letters at a time, sliding each tile across the board, changing direction if Grandma's eye ticked or Mum bit her lip. They were pretending that each of their words was the most important, ever, but they weren't especially cool ones. I mainly watched the clock hands, creeping towards perfect alignment. I told them it was six o'clock, but Grandma was celebrating her high-scoring N1A1Z10I1, and had forgotten all about the news.

Eventually, the bag was empty. All the blanks were gone. Mum and Grandma were fiddling with their last few tiles, staring at the board. I had seven letters left to play. I had collected them. They were the ones I wanted. I put down E1Q10U1I1N1O1X8 with the X8 on the triple score supergiant corner square. I said it aloud, though nobody had asked me to, and I told them that it was my top favourite word and explained what it meant.

That night I watched Star Trek from the sofa.

ABOUT THE HYSTERECTOMY ASSOCIATION

The Hysterectomy Association provides impartial, timely and appropriate information and support to women. It was founded in the mid 1990's by Linda Parkinson-Hardman who is the author of several books about hysterectomy, online business and one novel.

It is based in Dorset in the UK and you can find out more about the association through the following accounts:

Website: hysterectomy-association.org.uk
Facebook: facebook.com/HysterectomyUK
Twitter: twitter.com/HysterectomyUK
LinkedIn: linkedin.com/company/the-hysterectomy-association

Other books from The Hysterectomy Association include:

- 101 Handy Hints for a Happy Hysterectomy
- In My Own Words: Women's Experience of Hysterectomy
- Losing the Woman Within
- The Pocket Guide to Hysterectomy
- A Diva's Guide to the Menopause - Short Story
- Hysteria 1
- Hysteria 2
- Hysteria 3
- Hysteria 4
- Hysteria 5

You can connect directly with Linda, our editor, on her blog at womanontheedgeofreality.com.

www.ingramcontent.com/pod-product-compliance
Lightning Source LLC
Chambersburg PA
CBHW070802120626
46557CB00002B/688